Fish Girl

Story by Donna Jo Napoli
& David Wiesner
Pictures by David Wiesner

CLARION BOOKS • NEW YORK

SEE THE MYSTERIOUS
FISH GIRL
WHO IS SHE ?
IS SHE
BREATHES UNDERWATER— BUT LIVES LIKE A GIRL!
SHOWS
1:00 & 3:00
$2.00

Welcome to Ocean Wonders, the realm of Neptune, god of seas and storms! I am the most powerful of the gods. All life began in the watery depths, where I reign supreme. Everything you see here obeys my command. Behold! In every room of this house, you see the most amazing creatures of my kingdom. I have gathered them from across the oceans and seas for you to gaze upon!
VISIT
OCEAN
WONDERS
DAILY: 10AM - 6PM

Here you'll find specimens from the farthest corners of the earth. Strange beasts from the deepest, darkest depths, where no human has ventured—but where I, Neptune, travel with ease!

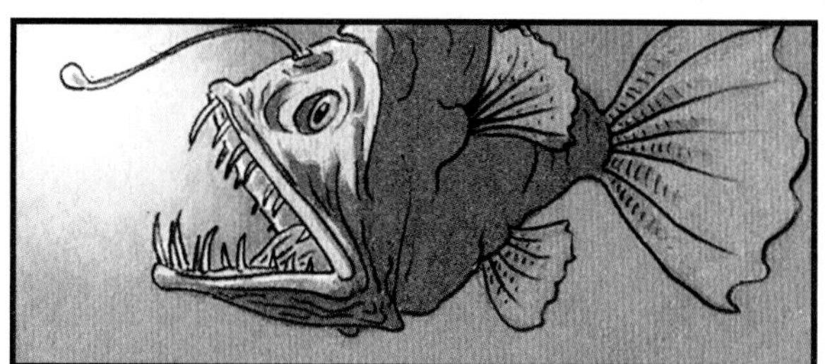

Creatures that are fearsome! ...beautiful!...grotesque! Creatures to amaze and delight child and adult alike!

Fish of every color, every size, and every shape!

Nowhere else will you see such extraordinary sights. Only here at Ocean Wonders!

And yet, as incredible as these denizens of the deep are, one transcends them all...

The Fish Girl! She is the mystery that lives in that lovely room. Look at her beautiful dresses and jewelry—all underwater! The Fish Girl! What is she? Is she fish or is she girl? You are fortunate to be here, for she is the last of her kind, and she can be seen only at Ocean Wonders!
FG

She is very shy, so you'll have to look for her. Watch carefully, and maybe you'll catch a glimpse.

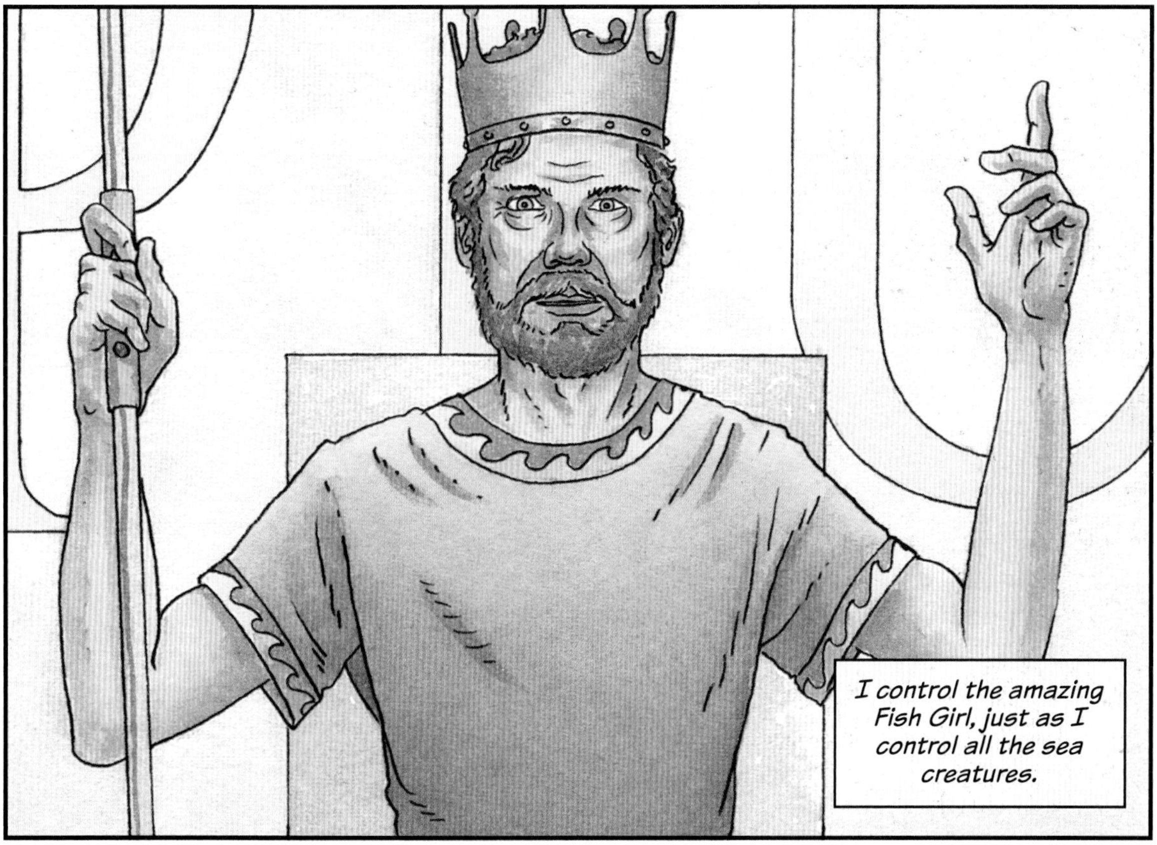

I control the amazing Fish Girl, just as I control all the sea creatures.

NEPTUNE
I am god of the seas! I am Neptune!

Never anger me, because you risk seeing what I can do.

One swing of my trident drives winds into frenzied shrieks. One swing stirs whirlpools, shipwrecks sailors...turns a burbling stream into a raging, racing flood!

I, Neptune, can bring disaster to those who defy me—so always respect and honor the god of the seas!

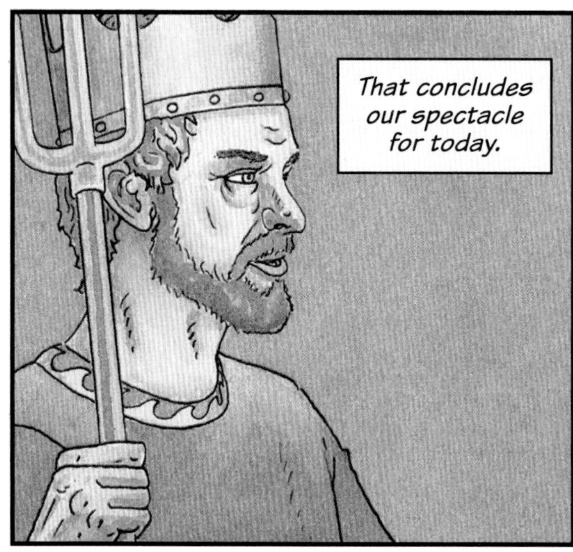
That concludes our spectacle for today.

But don't leave empty-handed...

The gift shop has many wonderful items for— Wait...what? This part is new!
IN ADDITION TO ALL THE REGULAR ITEMS IN THE GIFT SHOP, WE'RE OFFERING YOU A SPECIAL TREAT—A T-SHIRT TO HELP YOU REMEMBER WHAT YOU SAW HERE TODAY!
FISHGIRL

Business must be bad if he's changing his routine.

He's always worried about money.

Beautiful fish aren't enough for the humans.
TEN BUCKS?
NEPTUNE

They want the big mystery— the Fish Girl.

Where is the Fish Girl?

What is the Fish Girl?

Who is the Fish Girl?

I am the Fish Girl.

You're happy they're all gone, aren't you, Herring?

I'm always happy when they leave.

I want to see that new T-shirt.

GIFT SHOP
Is that supposed to be me?

What was he thinking?

Oh!

WAIT...
DON'T GO!

Oh, no! She saw me! How could I be so careless? That's Neptune's most important rule!

THERE YOU ARE! I WAS ALL THE WAY DOWNSTAIRS.
I SAW HER!

YOU'RE NOT SUPPOSED TO BE UP HERE AFTER THE SHOW ENDS.
I SAW THE MERMAID!

LIVIA, YOU'RE TOO OLD FOR THAT NON-SENSE.
MOM, I'M SERIOUS!

SHE HAD A TAIL AND EVERYTHING! FOR REAL!
SHE'S BEAUTIFUL.

She's gone... Neptune will be furious.

Octopus, did you see that girl? Did you hear her? Come on, fast, before they leave.

The mother's angry. She doesn't believe the girl.

Good. They mustn't say anything to Neptune about me. Oh, please...

There he is...they see him...they're walking past him. I'm safe for now.
She called me beautiful. Will she come back? I sort of want her to.

But humans are dangerous. And one of them has seen all of me, not just the little bits I'm supposed to let them see.

Maybe they'll call the police. Oh, I hope the girl can't convince her mother.

She probably can't. Parents never believe. They always say "Mermaids aren't real," or "You should know better," or "Act your age." And kids say "I did too see her!" or "She waved at me!" That's what kids say. They want to believe.

Sometimes they say "She's a fake" or "She's a freak." I hate that word, Octopus.
But that girl didn't seem scared, did she? She smiled.

LOOK!

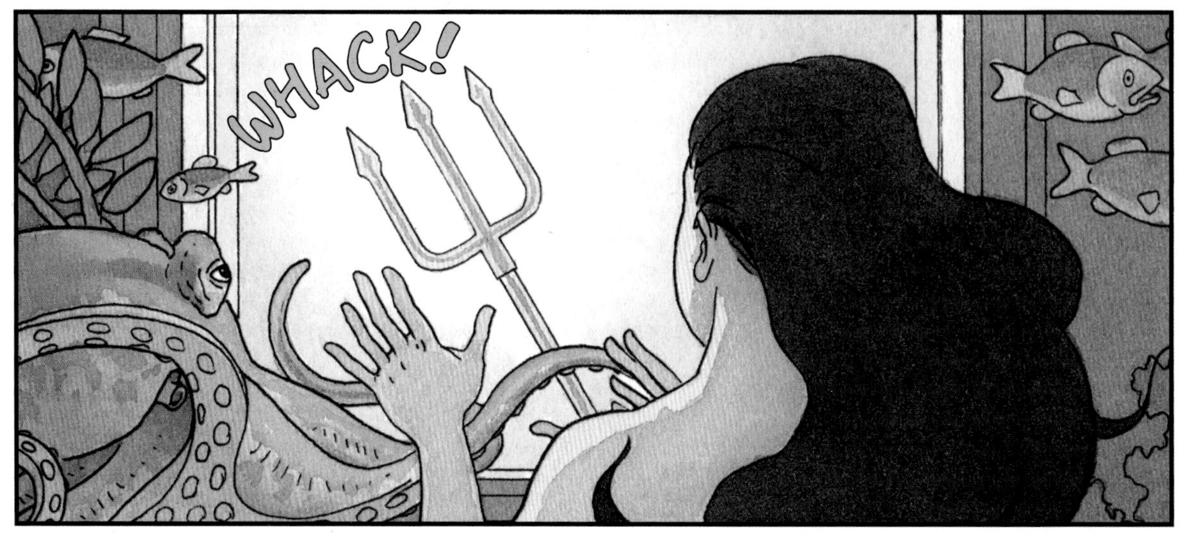
WHACK!

Oh! Someone outside saw me—and Neptune knows! I broke another rule.

"Stay away from the windows in daytime." He'll be so mad at me. Thank goodness he doesn't know about that girl.

He wants to protect me, but I wish he wouldn't scold me.

WHAT WERE YOU DOING, PRESSING UP AGAINST THE WINDOW LIKE THAT? ANYONE COULD HAVE SEEN YOU! NOT JUST THOSE KIDS—ADULTS!

IF THEY SEE WHAT YOU REALLY ARE, ALL THIS ENDS! YOU HAVE TO REMAIN A MYSTERY—YOU KNOW THAT.

THEY'LL CALL THE POLICE.

THEN THE SCIENTISTS WILL TAKE YOU TO A LAB.

YOU'LL BE A SPECIMEN. THEY'LL CUT YOU OPEN!
Stop!

THEY'LL BE REPULSED BY YOU.

But she said I was beautiful.

ARE YOU LISTENING TO ME?
EVEN THOUGH YOU'VE GROWN LUNGS ALONG WITH YOUR GILLS, YOU ARE NOT HUMAN! YOU'RE NOTHING LIKE THEM.

LISTEN. YOU ARE MINE. MY TREASURE. I'M THE ONE WHO CARES FOR YOU.
It's true.

DON'T LET THOSE LUNGS FOOL YOU. YOU BREATHE AIR, BUT YOU DON'T TALK.
NOW DO YOUR JOB. COLLECT THE COINS.

YOU'RE NOT HUMAN. NEITHER AM I. THE FISH GIRL AND THE SEA GOD. WE BELONG TOGETHER.

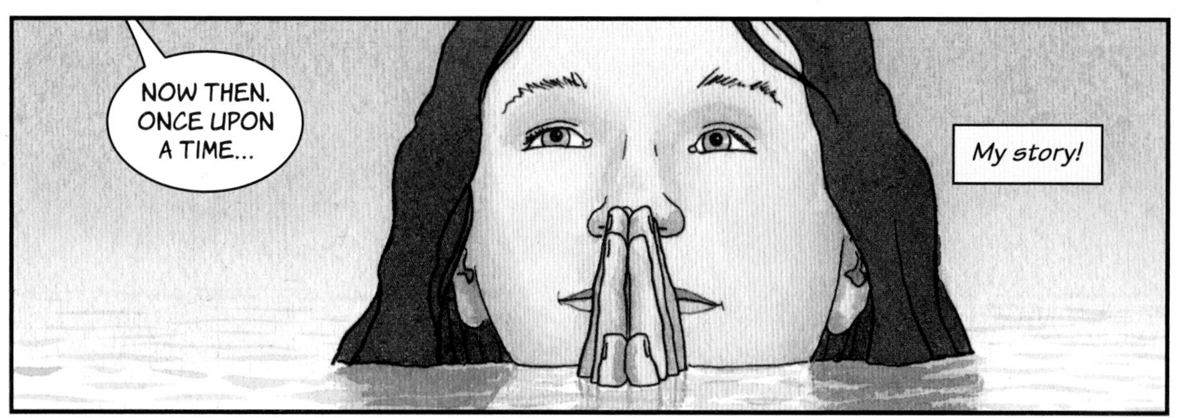

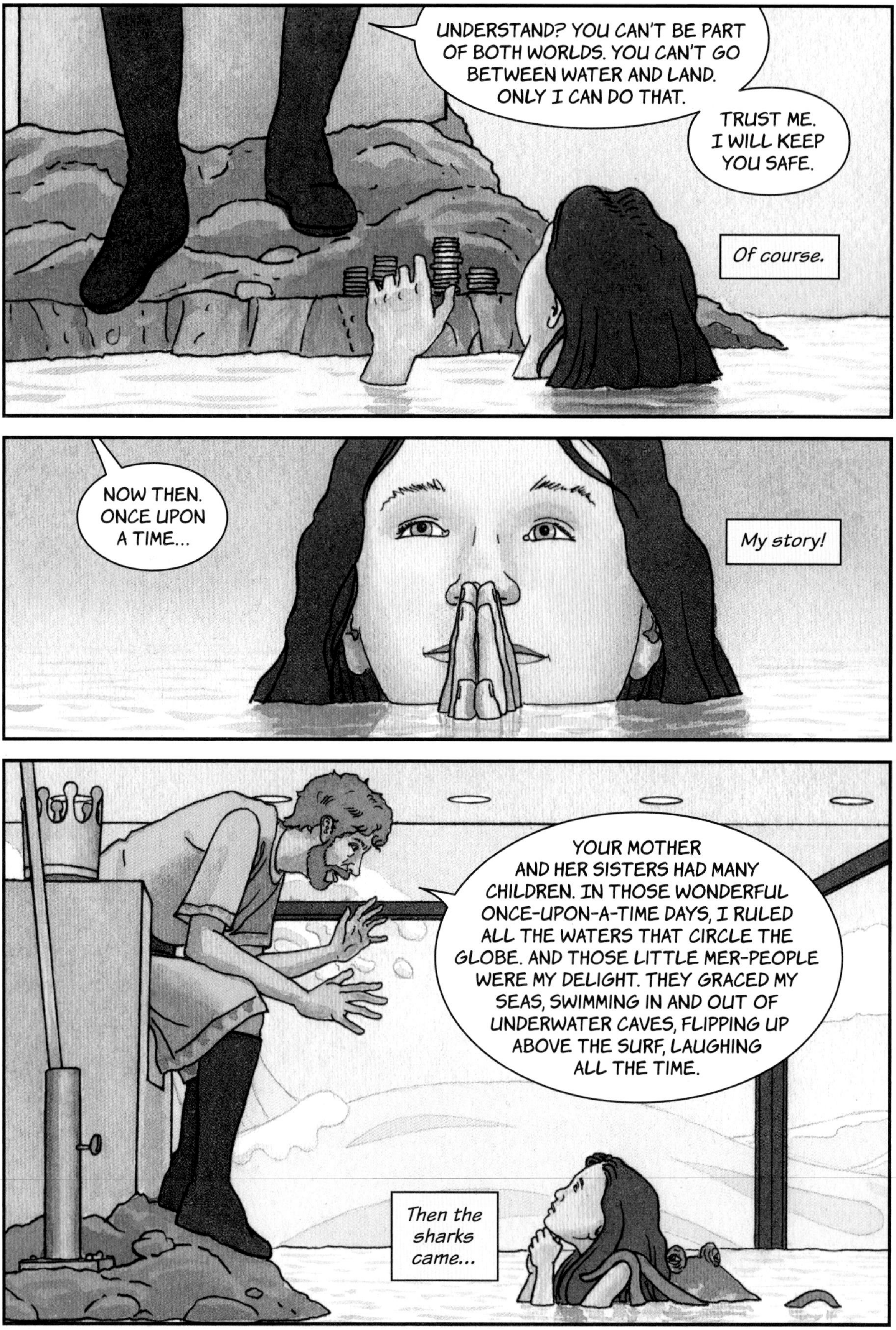

YOUR MOTHER AND HER SISTERS HAD MANY CHILDREN. IN THOSE WONDERFUL ONCE-UPON-A-TIME DAYS, I RULED ALL THE WATERS THAT CIRCLE THE GLOBE. AND THOSE LITTLE MER-PEOPLE WERE MY DELIGHT. THEY GRACED MY SEAS, SWIMMING IN AND OUT OF UNDERWATER CAVES, FLIPPING UP ABOVE THE SURF, LAUGHING ALL THE TIME.

Then the sharks came...

THEN THE SHARKS CAME. AND THE HUMANS IN BOATS WITH SPEARS AND NETS. EVIL MEN. EVERYTHING CHANGED. EVERYTHING WAS RUINED. ALL THE MER-PEOPLE, GONE.

EXCEPT YOU. I HID YOU. BABY YOU. I HELD YOU IN MY ARMS.
REMEMBER?
I do.

Arms around me is all I can remember before this tank.
Neptune's arms.

I BROUGHT YOU HERE, WHERE IT'S SAFE. I MADE THIS WORLD WHERE THE WICKED HUMANS CAN'T GET YOU.
THIS IS MY KINGDOM. AND YOUR HOME. NEVER FORGET THAT!

GET SOME REST.

GOOD NIGHT, MY TREASURE.

Neptune is right, isn't he, Octopus?

We don't need anyone else.

But still, I wonder what it would be like to swim in the ocean. Or talk.

What would it be like to make friends who aren't sea creatures... maybe those kids out there? What would we tell each other? But I love my sea friends. Oh, I love you. I love all of you.

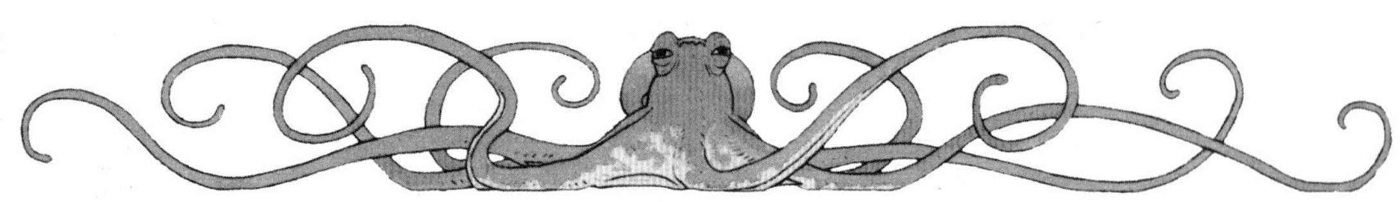

Today he's working on the filter.

What if he weren't here to fix it? He controls my world. My air. My food.

If the shark weren't fed, would it come after me?
Yes, Octopus, I know you'd protect me!

TIME TO OPEN. GO PLAY YOUR GAME.
People pay so they can try to spot me.

It's up to me to keep them coming back. To keep us alive.

Neptune does his part. I do mine.

COME IN.
SHE'S FRISKY
TODAY.
YEAH,
RIGHT.

YOU SEE
ANYTHING?
NAH.
HEY! A
SLUG!
They don't see all
the beautiful sea
creatures right in
front of their eyes.

Okay, here
you go,
a peek.

THERE
SHE IS!
WHERE?
NO
WAY!

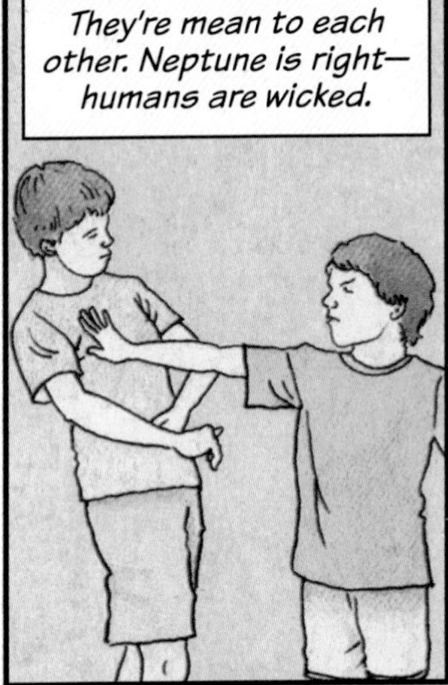
They're mean to each
other. Neptune is right—
humans are wicked.

Over here!

Missed me!

Here I am!

They don't care.

KEEP LOOKING! SHE'S TRICKY.
BOR... ING.

I wish I could show all of me and stop this game. It never ends in anything fun. They're so easy to fool.
Well, back to work. Oh, I can use Turtle as cover.

This is more of a challenge.

And the herrings.

It's her!
She's smiling.

I'm so glad
to see her.
I wish those kids
would go away.

Ha! I can lure them
downstairs...
SHE SWAM
DOWN!
YOU
BETTER BE
RIGHT!

...and come
back to peek.

Oh, she's gone!

She tricked me!

She's playing a game with me.

I'll wave back.

I like this game.

KEEP OUT

No! Don't go up there!

So many rules broken.

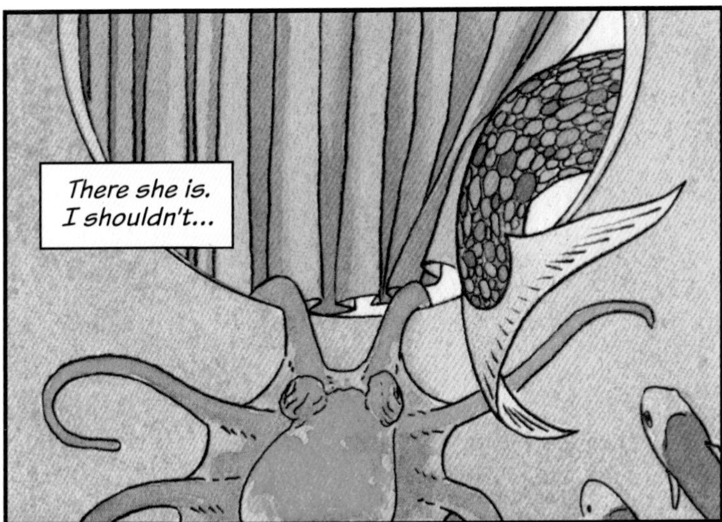
There she is. I shouldn't...

I KNEW YOU WERE REAL!

I MEAN, MOM THOUGHT I WAS CRAZY.

BUT I KNEW WHAT I SAW!

YOU UNDERSTAND ME, RIGHT? I CAN TELL!

Your voice is nice, like music.

WOW. YOUR FACE AND ARMS—YOU LOOK SO MUCH LIKE AN ORDINARY GIRL. LIKE ME! CAN YOU TALK?

Oh, I wish.

DID I SAY SOMETHING WRONG? DON'T BE SAD. YOU HAVE SUCH A PRETTY SMILE.
Relax, Octopus, we're safe. Don't get too big.

SEEMS LIKE THAT OCTOPUS REALLY LIKES YOU!

CAN YOU TALK TO THE FISH?

DO YOU EVER COME ALL THE WAY OUT OF THE WATER?

DO YOU HAVE LEGS INSIDE YOUR TAIL LIKE IN THE MERMAID STORIES?
Legs? In my tail?

LISTEN, I DON'T WANT TO SCARE YOU, BUT CAN I PLEASE TOUCH YOU? I'LL REACH REAL SLOW...

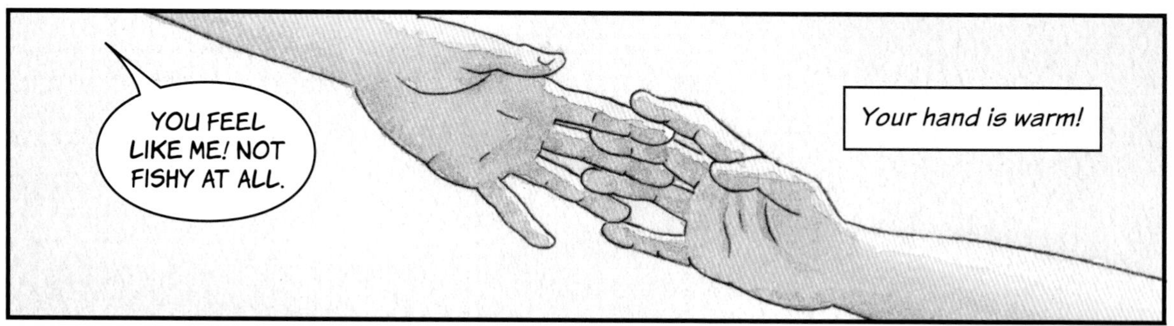
YOU FEEL LIKE ME! NOT FISHY AT ALL.
Your hand is warm!

CAN WE BE FRIENDS?
Friends?

DO YOU HAVE OTHER FRIENDS?
I have Octopus. And Turtle. I have the fish. But no one like you.

WHAT ABOUT THAT NEPTUNE GUY? OR IS HE YOUR DAD? ARE YOU A PRISONER HERE?
PTUNE
No! Neptune takes care of me.

I HAD A BIRTHDAY IN MAY. I'M TWELVE NOW. HOW OLD ARE YOU? WHEN'S YOUR BIRTHDAY?
Birthday?

YOU LOOK LIKE YOU'RE MY AGE. HERE— TAKE THIS! IT'S A CHARM FROM MY BIRTHDAY BRACELET.
IT REALLY RINGS— TRY IT!

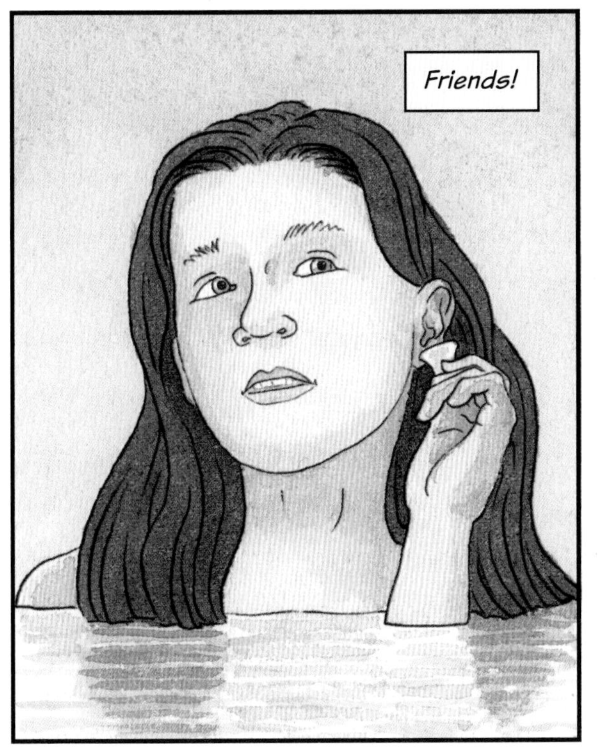
Friends!

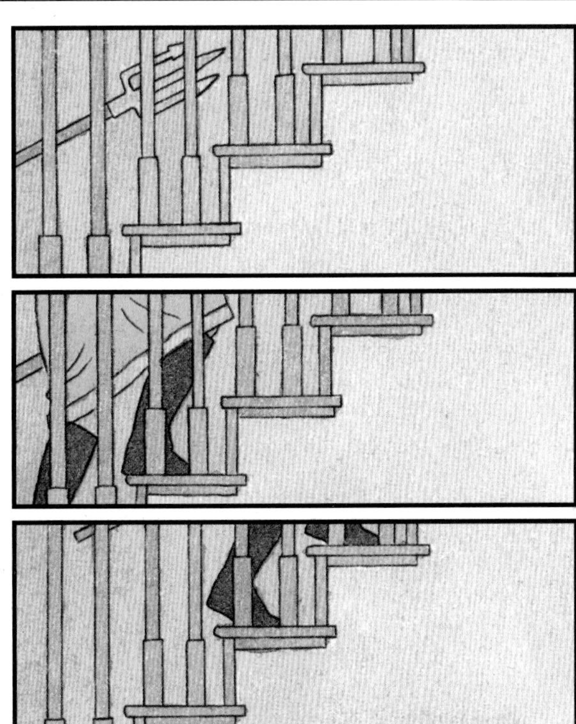

YOU'RE HIS SECRET. BUT NOW YOU'RE MINE, TOO. COULD YOU— OH!
Neptune's coming!

WHAT ARE YOU DOING? YOU'RE NOT ALLOWED UP HERE!
WHY NOT?

Please don't tell.

WHY NOT? THAT'S THE RULE—MY RULE!
BUT THERE'S SO MUCH TO SEE UP HERE.

WHAT DID YOU SEE?
TELL ME!

EVERYTHING!

EVERYTHING?

ALL THESE THINGS. YOU CAN SEE THEM BETTER FROM HERE.
DID YOU—
THOSE CONCHES ARE SO COOL!

MOST PEOPLE LIKE THE TIGER SHARK AND THE KEMP'S RIDLEY—THE BIG SEA TURTLE. THEY'RE NOT INTERESTED IN WHAT'S UP HERE.
OH, I AM. THOSE ARE SEA URCHINS, RIGHT?

THEY ARE! THEY HAVE TEETH, AND THEY EAT THE SEA KELP.
TEETH!

IF YOU PUT YOUR HEAD UNDERWATER, YOU CAN HEAR THEM MUNCHING.

HOW FUNNY.

Her laugh sounds like the bell. It's wonderful.

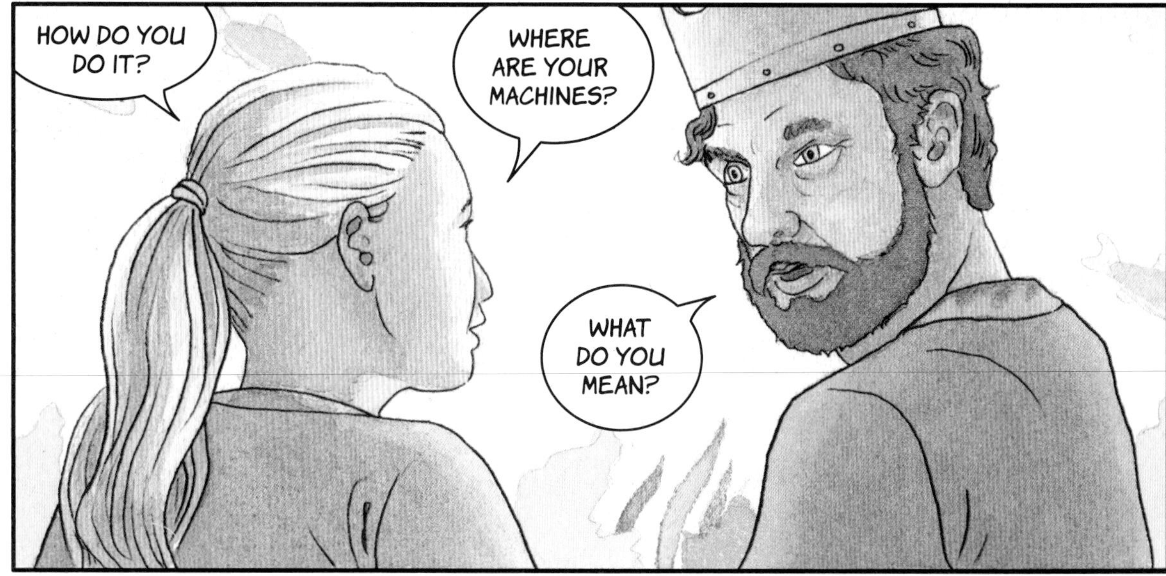
HOW DO YOU DO IT?
WHERE ARE YOUR MACHINES?
WHAT DO YOU MEAN?

I SAW YOUR SHOW. YOU MADE WAVES AND THUNDER.
I AM NEPTUNE, GOD OF SEAS AND STORMS!

OH, COME ON. I'M NOT A LITTLE KID. THE SHOW WAS REALLY GOOD.

WELL... TRICKS OF THE TRADE.

"Tricks of the trade"? What does that mean?

DOES SOMEONE TURN ON A WAVE MACHINE FOR YOU?
I WORK ALONE.

AND THE SOUND EFFECTS—THAT'S ANOTHER MACHINE, RIGHT?
OH, I KNOW! YOU HAVE A REMOTE CONTROL!
HA! ENOUGH! YOU CAN'T KNOW ALL MY SECRETS.

Secrets? What secrets? Neptune doesn't need machines to control the sea. He's a god.

OKAY. I HAVE TO GO. BUT I'LL BE BACK SOON.
ANYTIME.

OH,
ONE MORE
THING—

YOU DON'T
STOP, DO
YOU?
WHAT?

WHAT ABOUT
THIS FISH GIRL?
I MEAN, YOU
DON'T REALLY
HAVE A MERMAID,
DO YOU?

YOU'RE RIGHT.
IT'S TIME FOR
YOU TO GO.

YEAH, WELL...I'LL BE BACK.
CERTAINLY. COME BACK OFTEN. BRING YOUR FRIENDS.

BUT STAY DOWNSTAIRS FROM NOW ON.
IT'S OFF-LIMITS UP HERE, EXCEPT AT SHOWTIMES.
GOT THAT?

Octopus, what just happened?

I HOPE MORE PEOPLE COME TOMORROW.
YOU NEED TO PLAY THE GAME BETTER. I CAN'T DO EVERYTHING.

I'M GETTING TOO OLD. TOO TIRED.

The girl said "machines." Neptune said "tricks." That's different, isn't it? I don't understand what they were talking about.

But Neptune seemed to like her...until she asked about me.

She said I looked like her—like an ordinary girl.

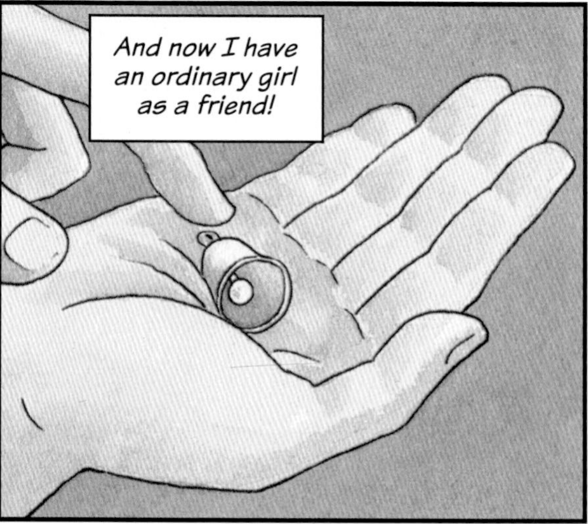
And now I have an ordinary girl as a friend!

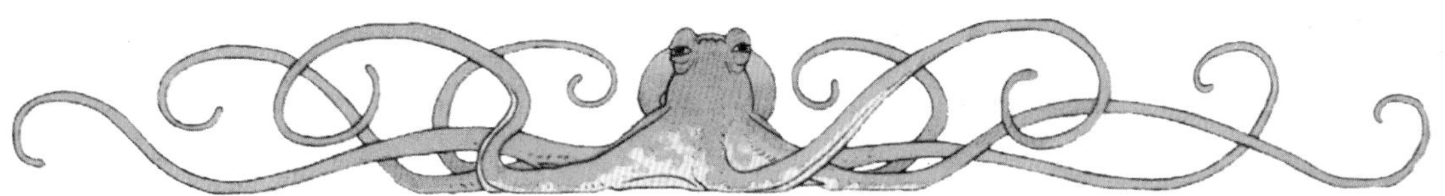

The doors are open!
She's coming today!
WONDERS
Daily 10 AM - 6 PM

It has to be today!
She said she'd
be back soon.

I don't see her.

Not here,
either.

I hate waiting.

IT'S HER!
LOOK!

Oh, no—he saw too much of me! Octopus, wave a leg!

IT'S AN OCTOPUS, KNUCKLE-HEAD.
I SAW THE MERMAID!
HA!
That was close. I'm tired of these kids. Always the same.
No more games today.

If I can find some unbroken shells, I can make a gift for that girl. It could be a necklace as pretty as the jewelry in my drawer.

They'd look good on her...on my friend.

Come, friends,
let's hide today.

I see people collecting shells.
I could find good shells out
there. Whole, not broken.

Look at them. They walk and talk
and run. They even swim. They
look happy...like it's all so easy.

I can't walk like them, but they can swim like me. It's not fair.

The humans act like they own the sea. But Neptune will reclaim it one day.
WELCOME TO OCEAN WONDERS—

Showtime. The same routine again and again.
NEVER ANGER ME, BECAUSE YOU RISK—
"Never anger me..." Always the same words. Like a machine.

Like a machine...

Livia said "machines." Does this control his waves?

Here it comes: "One swing—"
ONE SWING OF MY TRIDENT STIRS WHIRLPOOLS, SHIPWRECKS SAILORS!
CLICK! CLICK! CLICK!
MMMMMMMRRRRRRMMMMMM

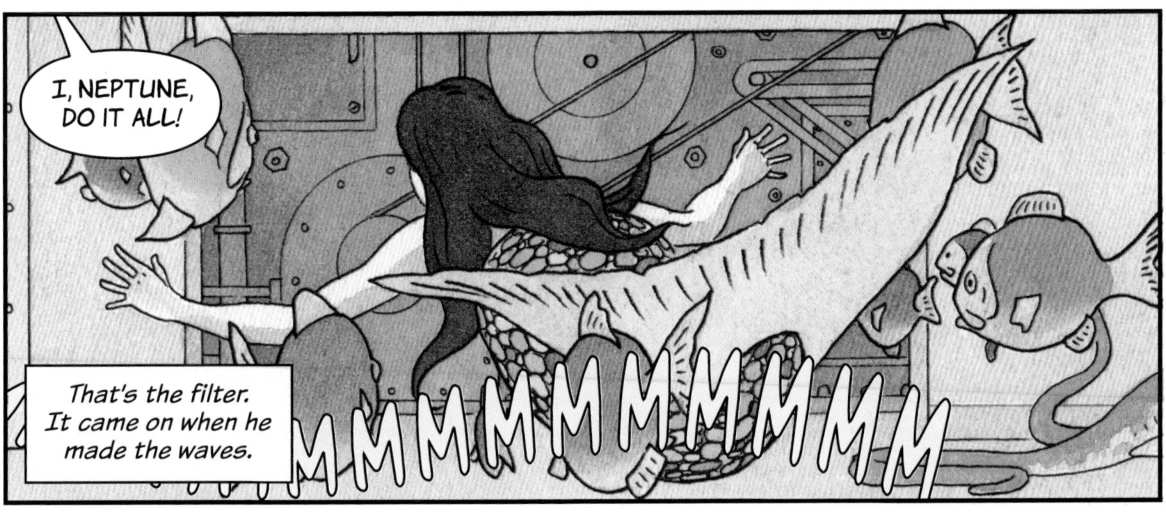
I, NEPTUNE, DO IT ALL!
That's the filter. It came on when he made the waves.
MMMMMMMMMMMM

THAT CONCLUDES OUR SPECTACLE FOR TODAY. THE GIFT SHOP IS OPEN—
He wouldn't lie to me.

YOU CAN COME OUT NOW.

I KNEW YOU WERE THERE. I ALWAYS KNOW WHERE YOU ARE.

WHAT A SLOW DAY!
AND YOU—FIRST YOU FLIT AROUND SO PEOPLE SEE TOO MUCH OF YOU...
AND THEN YOU HIDE ALL AFTER-NOON.

WHAT'S GOING ON?
YOU WERE RECKLESS.

DON'T COLLECT THE COINS—THERE AREN'T ENOUGH TO BOTHER WITH.
NO STORIES TONIGHT. I'M TIRED. I'M GOING HOME.

Home.
FISH GIRL
VISIT

This isn't Neptune's home. It's mine. At least at night.

Do ordinary girls have homes like this?

I'll put on a dress, the way ordinary girls do.

Neptune made this room for me.

He does everything for me. He'd never lie to me...
...would he?

There can't be machines, Octopus. There aren't any switches.
If there were machines, someone else would have to work them, and there's only me.

I KNOW! YOU MUST HAVE A REMOTE CONTROL!

Oh.

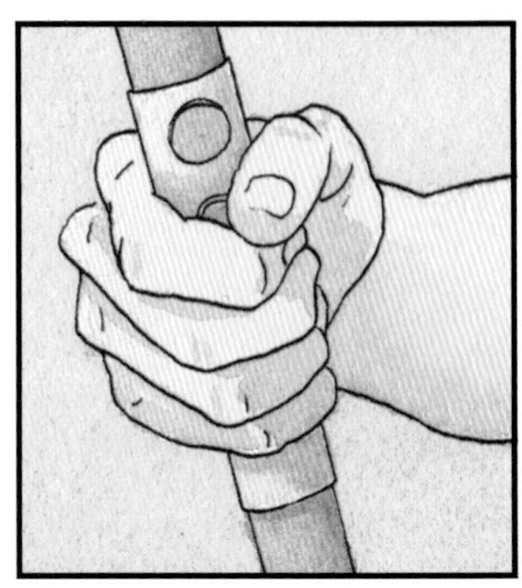

It must be the trident!

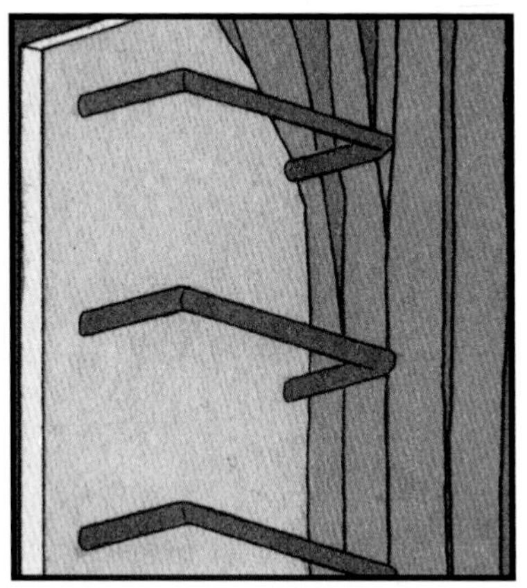

Okay.

I have to try,
Octopus.
I have to know.

I'm out! It feels strange...The air is all around me. It's so dry!

I'm heavy...so very heavy.
My tail weighs me down.

How do humans
move, out in the air?

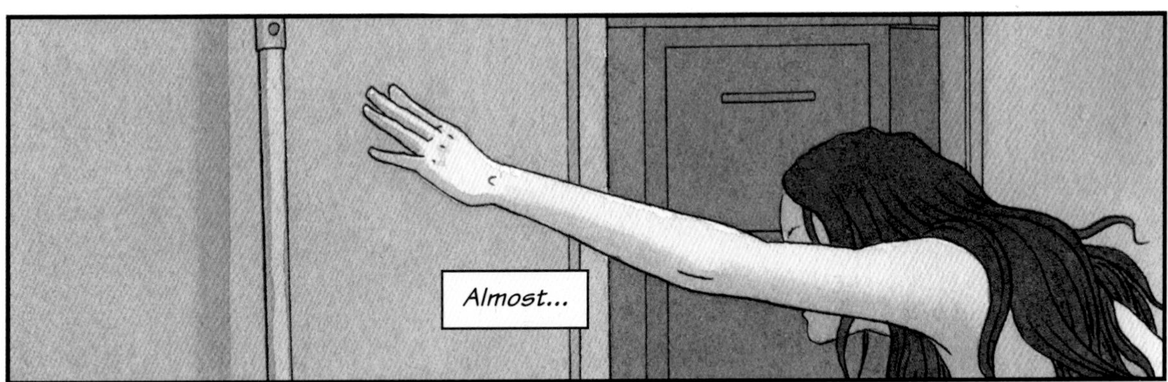
Almost...

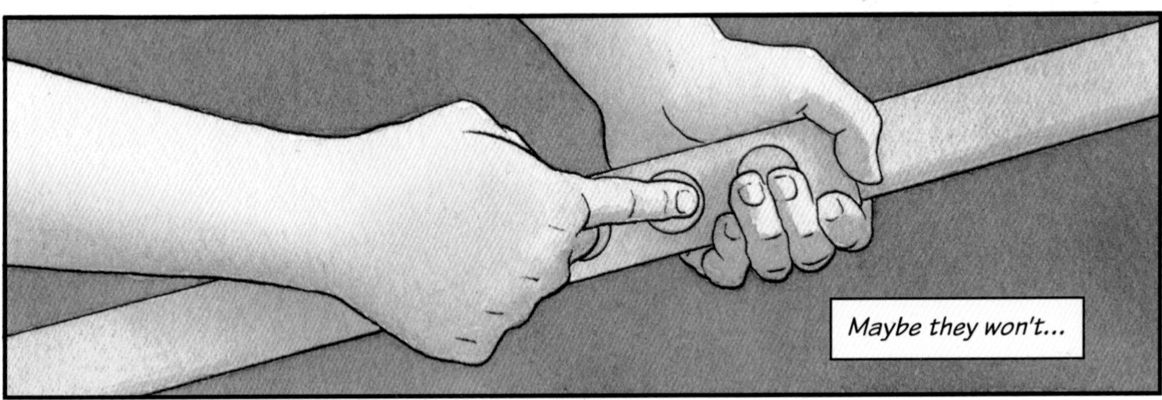
Maybe they won't...

MMMMMMMMMMMMMMM

He lied!
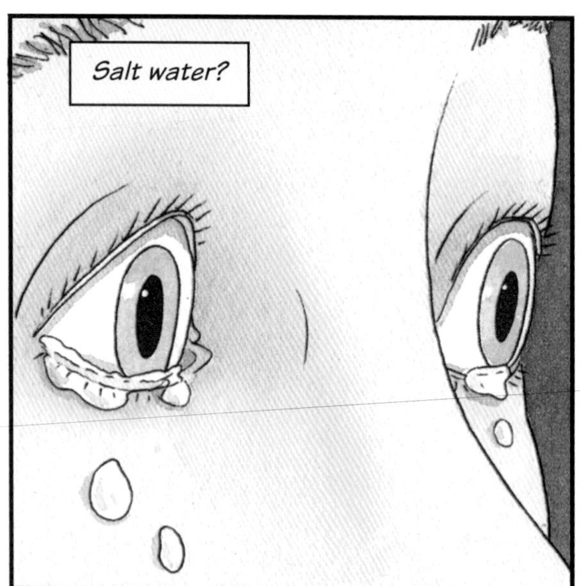
Salt water?

Tears! I've only cried underwater before.

Octopus, I'm scared.
You're scared too.
I'm coming...

Put this
back first.

I'm so dry,
I can barely
move.

My scales are
coming off!

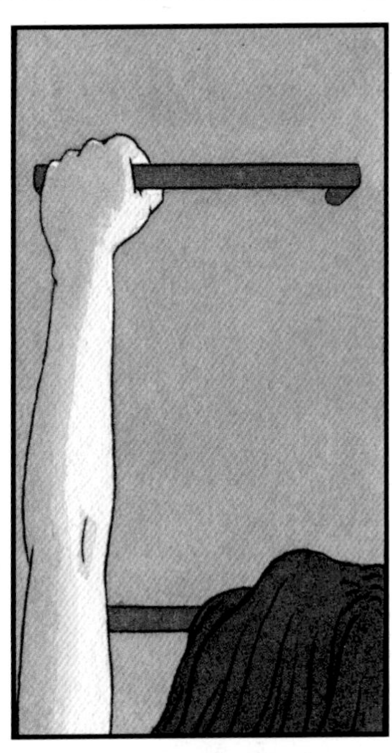

I can't climb in, Octopus.
Neptune will find me here.
This is worse than breaking
his rules. This is so bad, there
isn't even a rule against it.

Octopus,
pick me up.

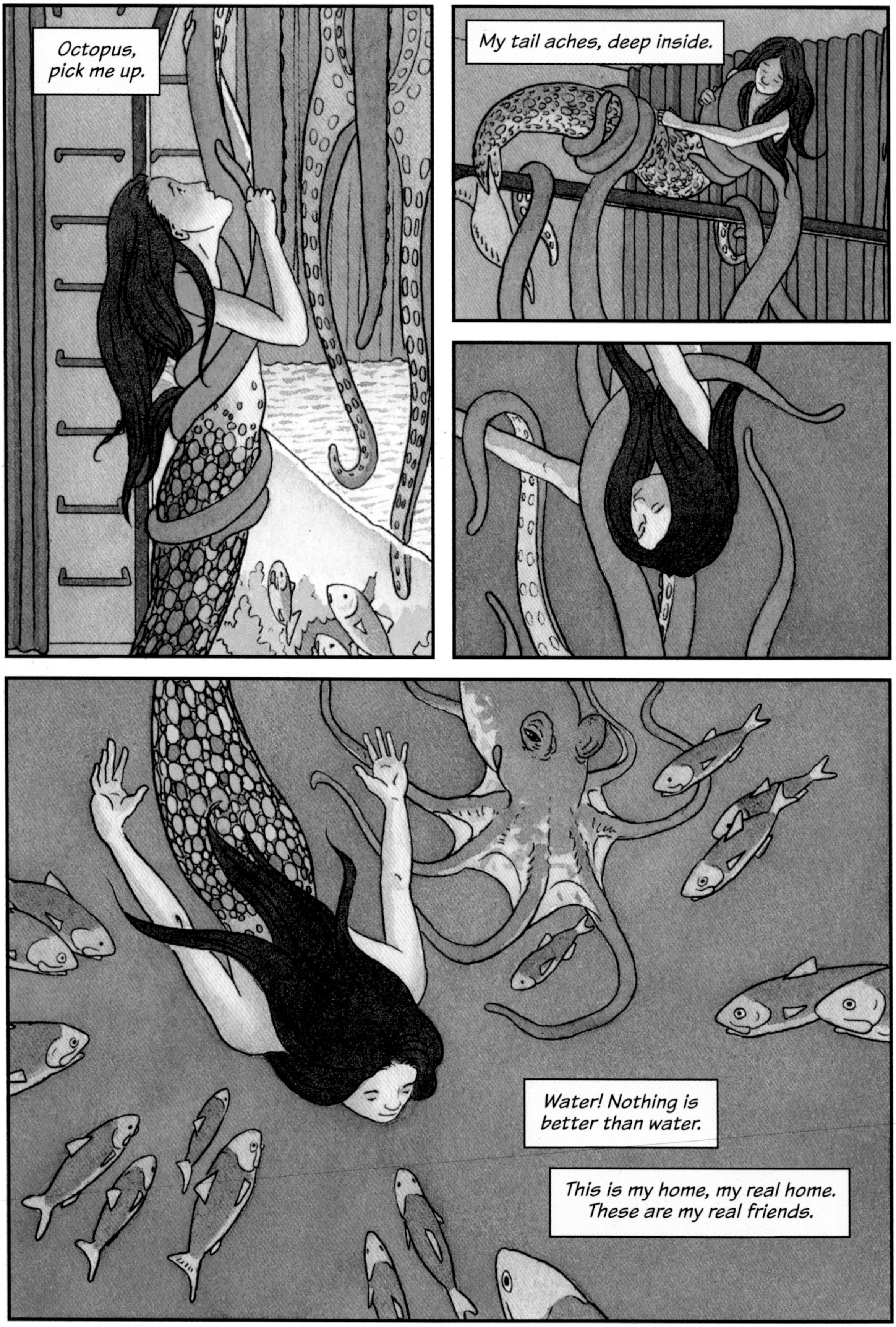

My tail aches, deep inside.

Water! Nothing is better than water.

This is my home, my real home. These are my real friends.

I feel good now, light and free and fast.

Except for that ache inside my tail.

Where is it? Ah...

Why would Neptune lie about controlling the waters?

Is this part of getting old, like he said? Is he losing his powers?

Who can I trust? Of course I trust you, Octopus. But what about the girl? I want to trust her. I do trust her.

So tired. I can't keep my eyes open.

This morning
feels different.

LOOK AT THAT RAY!
FORGET THAT STUPID RAY.

I SAW THE MERMAID LAST TIME.
SHE'S A FAKE. LET'S GO FIND THE EELS.

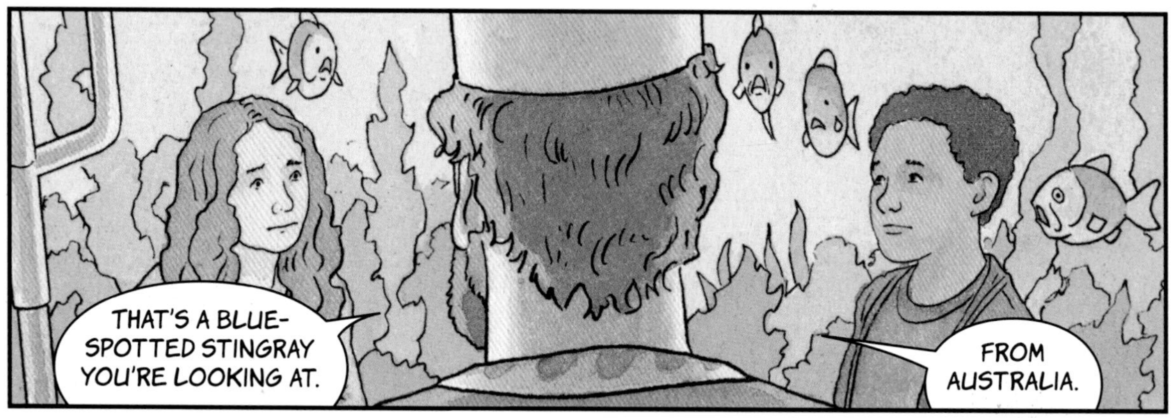
THAT'S A BLUE-SPOTTED STINGRAY YOU'RE LOOKING AT.
FROM AUSTRALIA.

IT'S NOT STUPID. LOOK IN ITS EYES. IT'S SMART.

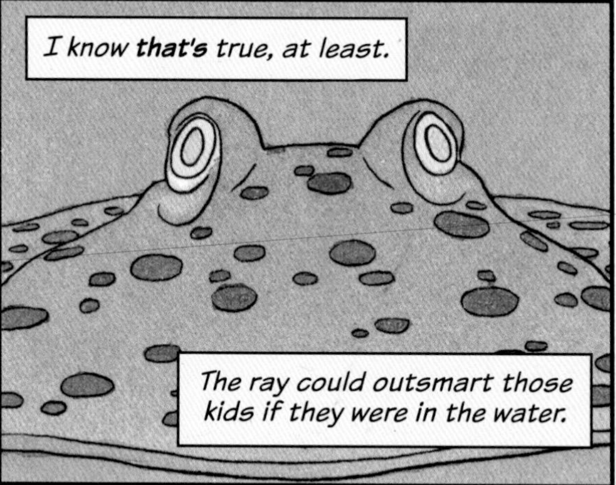
I know **that's** true, at least.
The ray could outsmart those kids if they were in the water.

MANY SEA CREATURES ARE SMART.

Including me?

My tail still aches. I must have hurt it last night.

Good—some whole ones for the necklace.

Time to do my job.

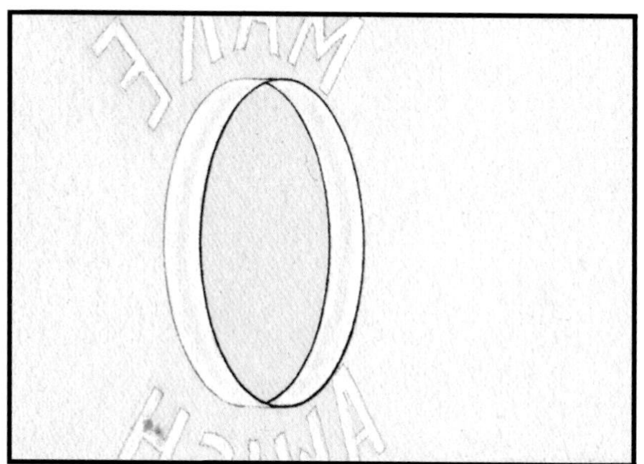

NEP
MAKE
A WISH

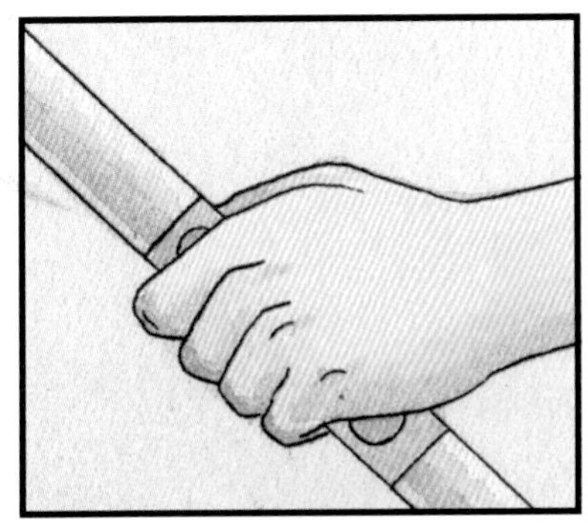

There it is.

YOU DID A GOOD JOB TODAY. EVERYONE THOUGHT THEY SAW YOU.

HMM... NOT BAD. YOU'VE EARNED A STORY TONIGHT.

I'LL TELL YOU HOW YOUR MOTHER AND HER SISTERS CAME TO BE—AND HOW THEY PERISHED.

I WASN'T THE ONLY GOD OF WATERS IN THOSE DAYS. THERE WAS A RIVER GOD. HE FATHERED THE MERMAIDS. THEIR MOTHERS WERE THE MUSES.

THE MUSES WERE LOVELY. THEY HAD THE FORM OF WOMEN, AND THEIR VOICES WERE SWEETER THAN ANYTHING ANYONE COULD EVEN DREAM OF.

Really? He's never told me this before.

THE MUSES GAVE THEIR MERMAID DAUGHTERS THE GIFT OF SONG. IT WAS MARVELOUS, HOW THEY SANG.
My mother sang? She had a voice?

THEY LIVED ON AN ISLAND THAT WAS TALL AND CRAGGY AND DANGEROUS. NEAR THE ISLAND WAS AN UNDERWATER REEF.

YOUR MOTHER AND HER SISTERS SANG SO WONDERFULLY THAT SAILORS GOT DRUNK ON THEIR SONGS.

You said I can't talk, but my mother could sing? She sang wonderfully?
Tell me!

WHAT? SAILORS, IS THAT WHAT YOU WANT TO KNOW ABOUT? THEY'RE JUST MEN WHO RIDE AROUND IN BOATS, LIKE FISHERMEN, BUT THEY DON'T FISH.
Tell me about my mother's songs.

STOP THAT! WHAT'S THE MATTER WITH YOU?
Tell me!
THAT'S IT— I'M GOING HOME.

VISIT
OCEAN
WONDERS
10 AM - 6 PM

At night, this
place is mine.

I don't have
to be careful.
No one is
looking for me.

My friends
and I are free.
For a while.

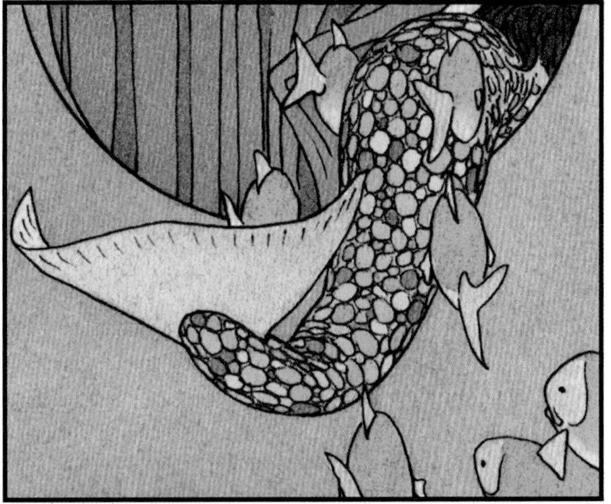

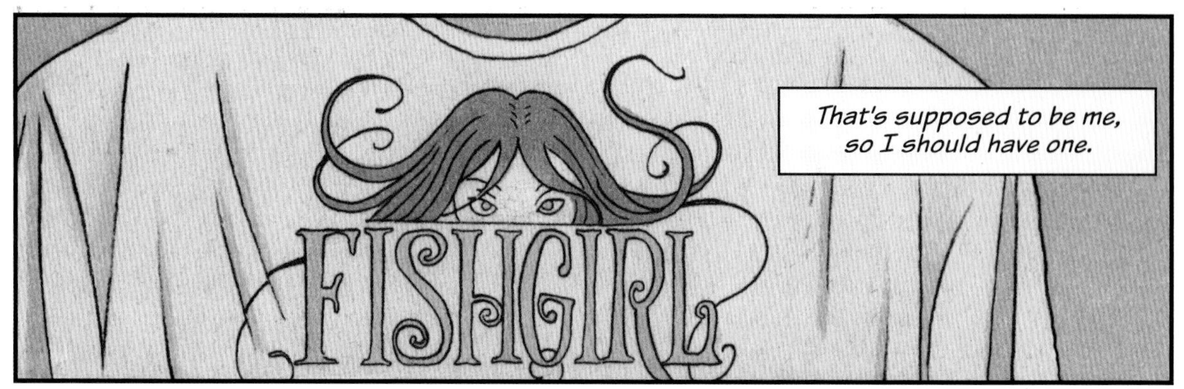
FISHGIRL
That's supposed to be me, so I should have one.

Hmm...if the floor was wet, I could slide.

Octopus, splash enough water over the rim so I can move across the floor out there.

Don't look at me like that. Why shouldn't I go out there? I did it before and nothing bad happened.
Please...won't you help me?

Oh, that's much better.

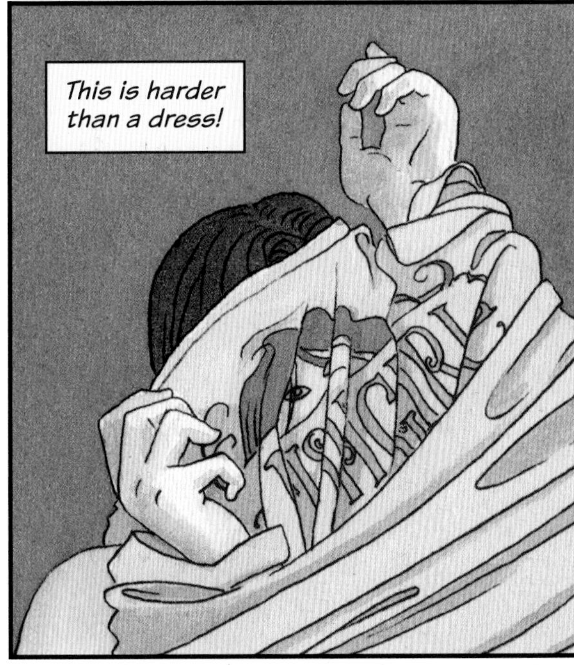
This is harder than a dress!

In this T-shirt I look
like a girl. I look human.
I look like someone who
can walk. And talk.
My mother sang.
My mother had a voice.
Do I?

. . .

Okay, I'm coming back.

What does he keep in there?

More secrets?

It's okay,
I'm just going
to look.

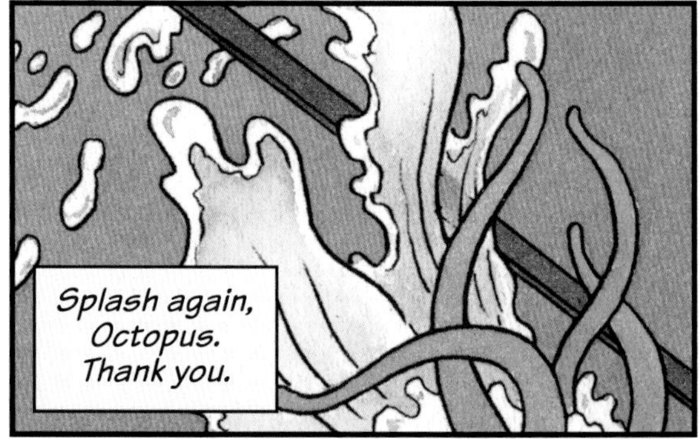
Splash again,
Octopus.
Thank you.

That ache is back.
Worse than before.

This was a mistake...

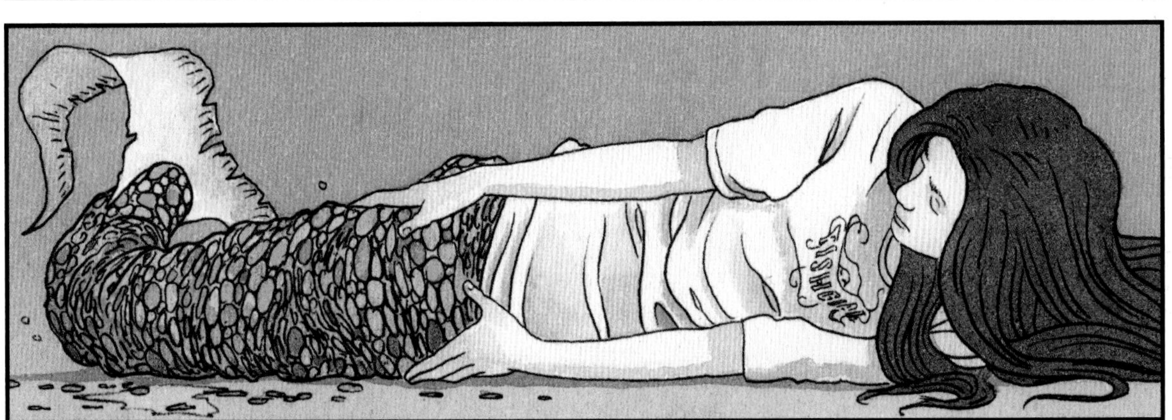

What's happening to me?

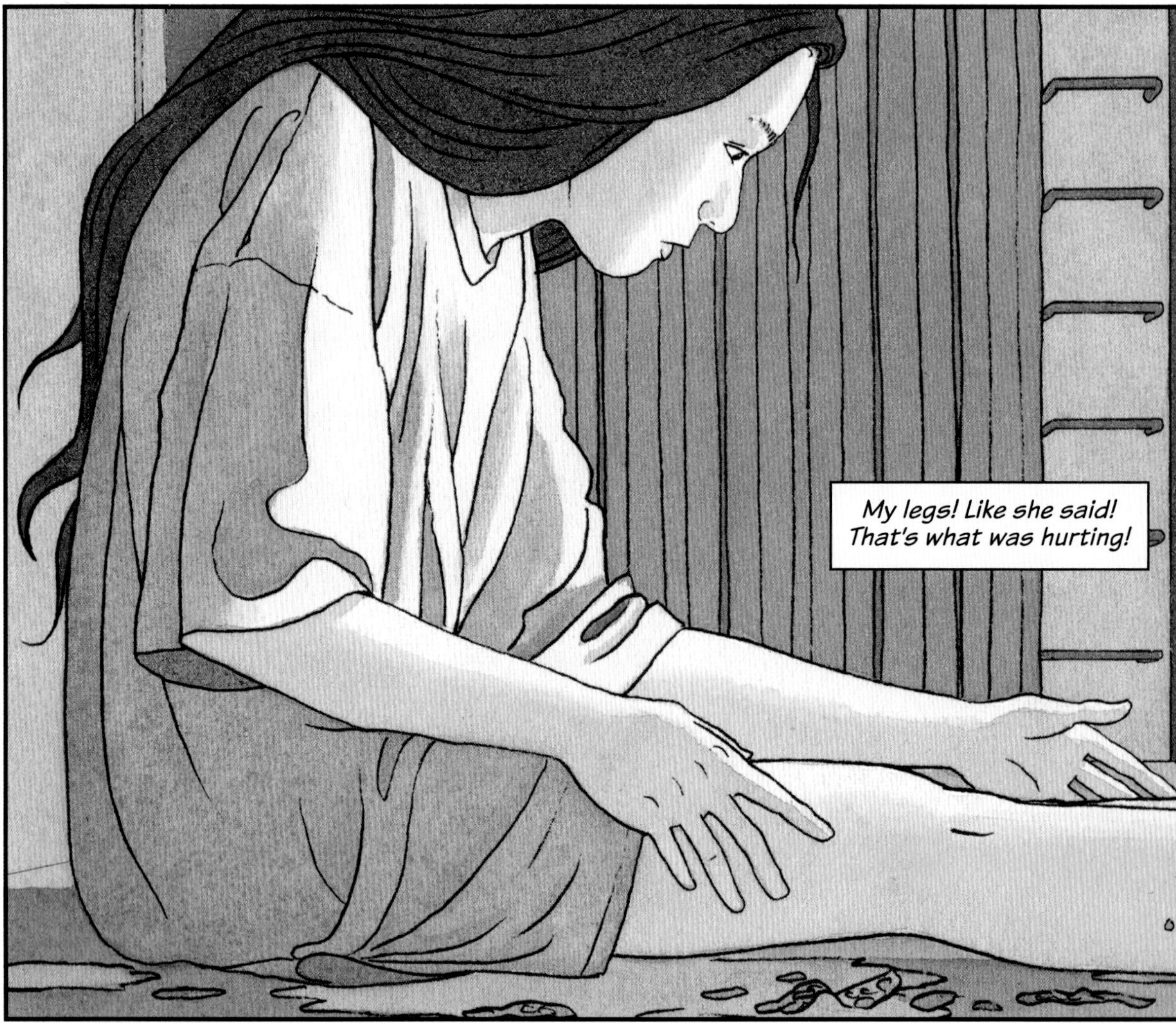

My legs! Like she said!
That's what was hurting!

Octopus...did you know about this? Neptune must know. Why didn't he tell me?

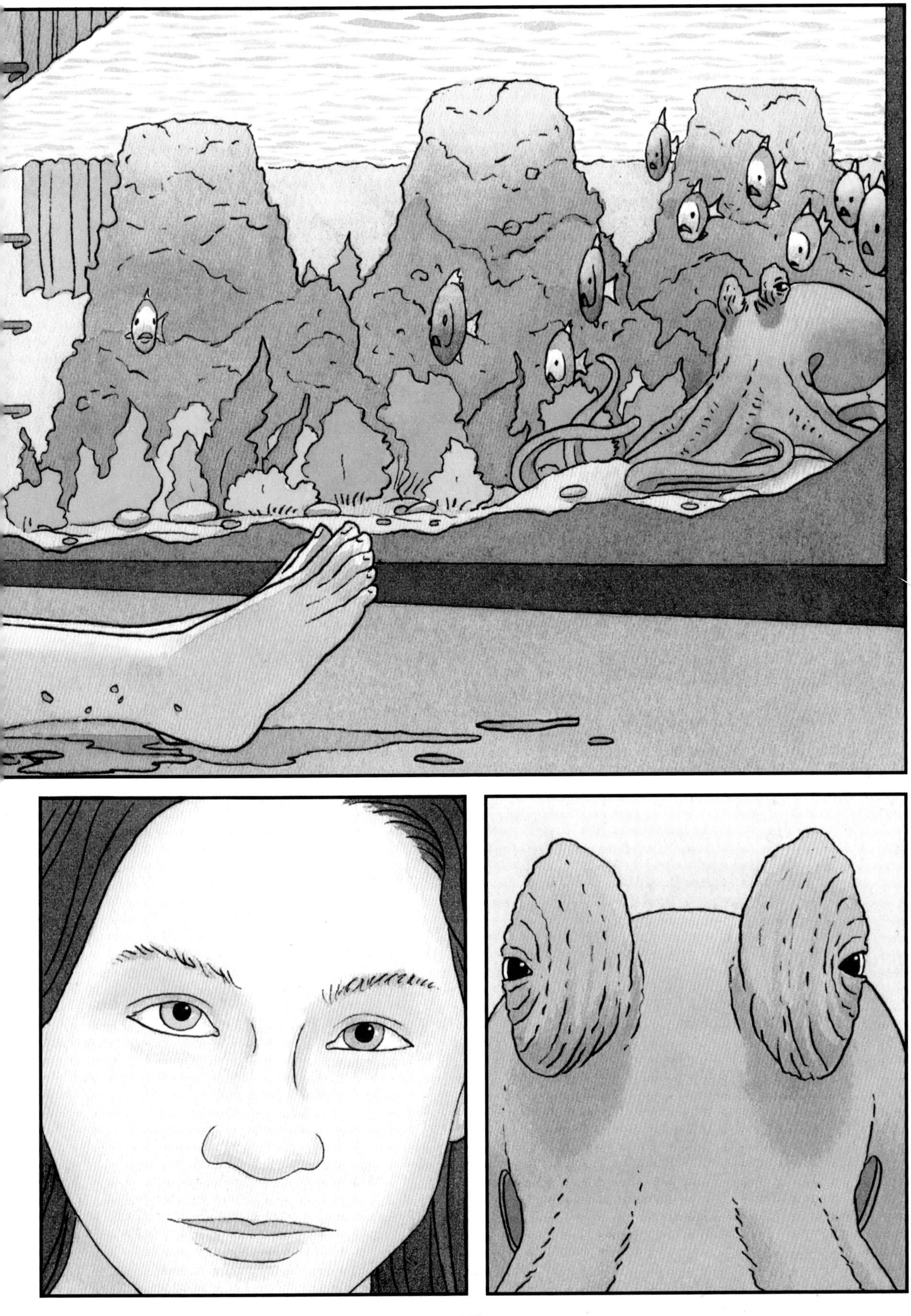

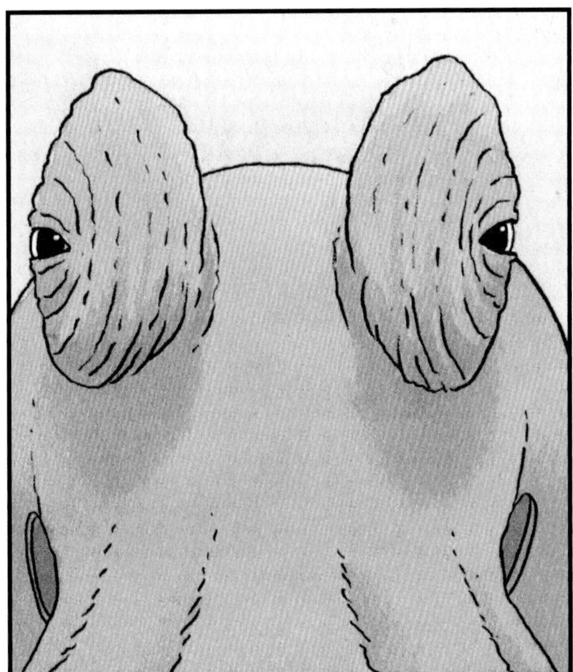

If I have legs,
I should be able
to walk.

How do I...?

Oof.

Ha! Look!
There's a girl
in the mirror!
Me!

I'm walking!

Me, with legs, walking!

Oh!

Air is coming in! Salt!
It tastes of fish.

It's so big out there!
What's that sound?
Whoosh, whisssh.
Again and again. My heart
beats in time with it.
Waves! Of course!
I can hear the sea
from here. I love it.

What are all those lights?
And those sounds?

Hey, funny seagull. Hey!

AHHH...

Okay, Octopus, I'm coming.

I've always loved seeing this light.

It's like an anglerfish glowing...

...while Neptune works on his "papers."

Ah! It's much brighter than an anglerfish.

WATER CO.
OVER DUE
WATER CO.
What does he do with all these things?

WATER CO.
OVER DUE
WATER CO.
So much paper.

Books! Are my stories in them?
PHOTOS

GRAND OPENING

I know some of these places! I see them from my windows. The ocean, the boardwalk...
FISHGIRL

FISH GIRL

Me. Fish Girl.
FISHGIRL

A boat...Who is that? Wait...It's Neptune!

He looks funny without his beard.

Neptune on a boat—is this when he still ruled the seas?

He's...
collecting
fish...

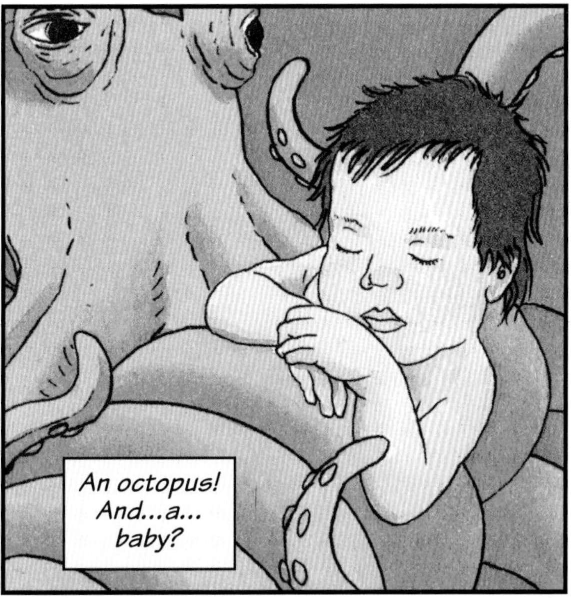
An octopus!
And...a...
baby?

ME!

Octopus and me.
Of course...the arms all
around me...that was
Octopus, not Neptune.

Neptune told my story the way he wanted, not the way it really was.

He lied...He was lying all along.

Neptune was a fisherman, not a god. He caught me. He set up this aquarium to make money off me.

What will he do if he finds me here with legs? His show will be ruined. I'm so tired.

Octopus...
thank you.

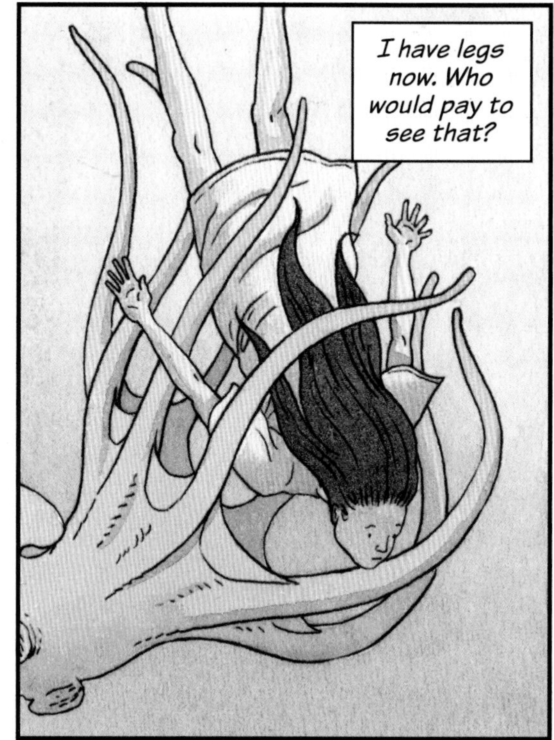
I have legs
now. Who
would pay to
see that?

Oh, my tail
again!
Good...I think.

I'm so confused.

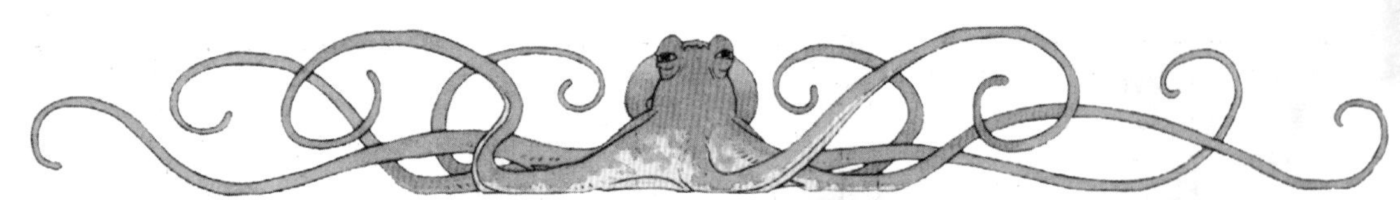

There he is.
The fisherman.

He's just a man who
presses buttons.

And tells lies.
Why should
I help him?

Here they come.
I'll hide here all day.
Me and you, Octopus.

HELLO?

PLEASE
COME
OUT!
My friend!

PLEASE. YOU HAVE TO BE THERE. MY MOTHER WON'T LET ME OUT OF HER SIGHT, NOT EVEN FOR A MINUTE. SHE'S GOT SO MANY PLANS FOR US THIS SUMMER.

IT'S LIKE SHE'S MY KEEPER.

Like Neptune. He's my keeper. I know that now.

THERE YOU ARE! I'M SO GLAD TO SEE YOU.
I KEEP THINKING ABOUT YOU. HOW DID YOU WIND UP IN THERE?
WHERE DID YOU COME FROM? I WISH YOU COULD TELL ME.

YOU'VE NEVER BEEN OUTSIDE, HAVE YOU? I'M GOING TO SHOW YOU MY WORLD.
I BROUGHT YOU SOME PICTURES I DREW.

THIS IS A SASSAFRAS TREE. YOU CAN SEE IT FROM MY WINDOW.
AND THIS IS A HORSE. I TAKE RIDING LESSONS ON SATURDAYS.
It's nothing like a seahorse.

DO YOU LIKE DRAWING? OH, I GUESS YOU CAN'T DRAW IN THERE.
Paper comes apart in water. I've seen it happen.
PAPER WOULDN'T WORK SO WELL IN WATER.

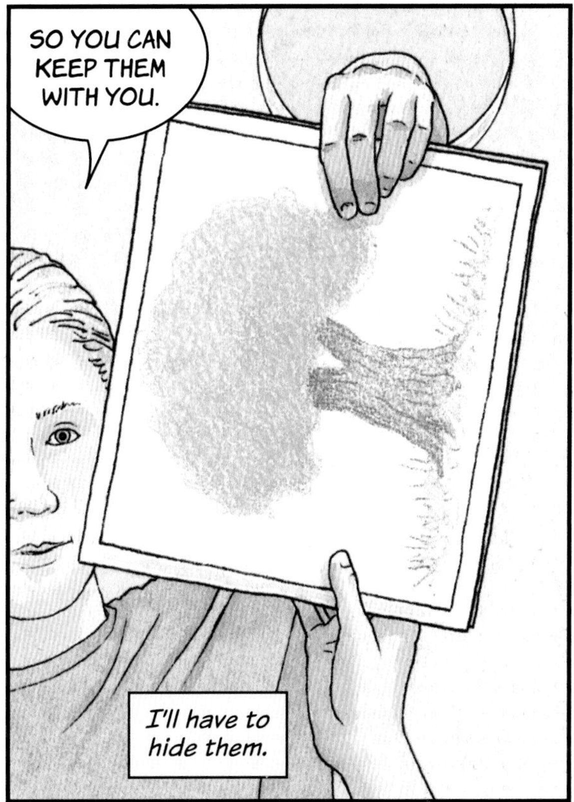

AND THIS IS MY DOG, WHACKY. I NAMED HIM THAT BECAUSE HIS TAIL WHACKS ON THE FLOOR WHEN HE'S HAPPY. I HAVE TO WALK HIM TWICE A DAY.

I've never heard anyone talk so much!

HE LIKES TO RIP THINGS UP. THIS IS HIS BABY DOLL. IT USED TO BE MINE, WHEN I WAS LITTLE, BUT HE CHEWED IT SO BAD, I GAVE IT TO HIM.

THIS IS MY BED. IT'S NOT AS FANCY AS YOURS. BUT I LIKE IT.

THIS IS A CHEESE AND LETTUCE SANDWICH. THAT'S CRAZY, HUH? I MEAN, WHO DRAWS A SANDWICH? BUT MAYBE YOU'VE NEVER SEEN ONE.

MY NAME IS LIVIA.
Liv-ee-uh.

DO YOU HAVE A NAME? IT CAN'T BE FISH GIRL, CAN IT?
Don't say that!

WOW, I'M SORRY!

HEY, WHAT IF I GIVE YOU A NAME?

What?

YOU'RE LIKE A MIRACLE. HOW ABOUT THAT? "MIRACLE"?

I HAVE TO GO.
I'M TAKING A YOGA
CLASS WITH MY MOM.
TO GET STRONG.

WE DO
THIS A LOT—
LOOK.
That makes
you strong?
MORE?
WELL, THERE'S
THIS...

AND THIS...

IT'S KIND
OF FUN. BUT
YOU NEED LEGS
TO DO IT.

SEE YOU
TOMORROW!

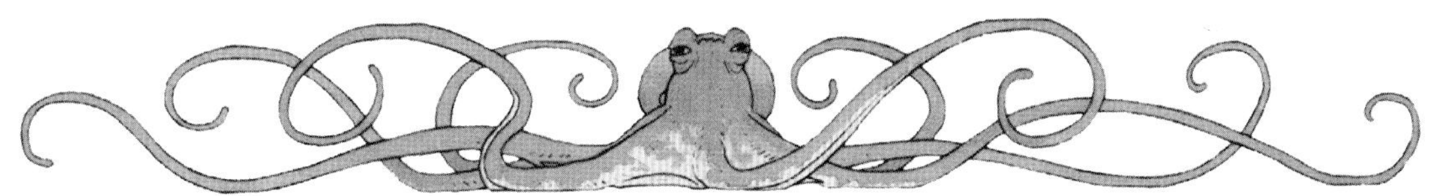

WHERE WERE YOU ALL DAY? I'M TALKING AND TALKING AND THERE'S NO SIGN OF YOU!

COME HERE, MY TREASURE.

NEP

THAT'S IT. UNTIL YOU BEHAVE, NO MORE STORIES.
COLLECT THE COINS. DO YOUR JOB!

My job now is to get strong.

FISHGIRL

AH... AH... AH...

IT'S PIZZA!

UH... UH... UH...

MAKE A WISH

FISHGIRL

AAH... AAH... AAH...

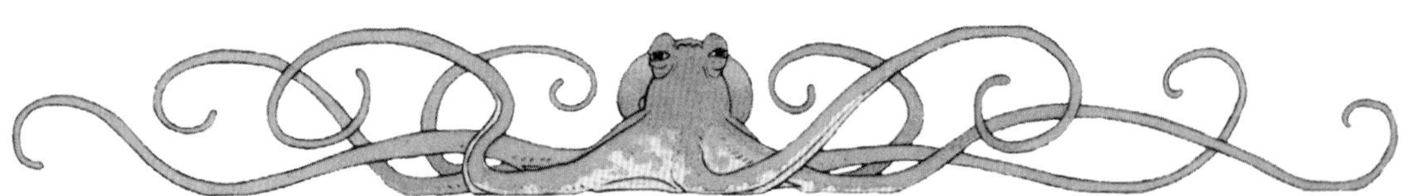

THIS REBELLION—OR TANTRUM OR WHATEVER IT IS—HAS GONE ON LONG ENOUGH.
NO ONE HAS SEEN YOU FOR DAYS. THEY'RE COMPLAINING.

WHAT'S WRONG WITH YOU?

YOU'VE CHANGED.

I MISS TELLING YOU STORIES.
BUT YOU HAVE TO EARN THEM. YOU HAVE TO BEHAVE.
GOOD NIGHT. LET TOMORROW BE A BETTER DAY.

I'm strong
enough now.
I hope.

Don't look at me like that—I can't tell if you're angry or scared.

I have to know what it's like out there. I'd take you with me if I could.

Oh! The air!
The salt!
The sea!

Everything glows...it's so clear without windows in the way. The waves seem like they're inside me, a part of me.

Oh, no... He'll call the police!

He must think I'm a real girl.

The sand is cool.

The air is never still.
FISHGIRL

The ocean keeps rolling in and slipping out. Like it's grabbing at the sand. Like it will grab at it forever and ever.

This water is...different. It's alive.

With my eyes closed, I feel like I'm somewhere else. Somewhere I almost remember.

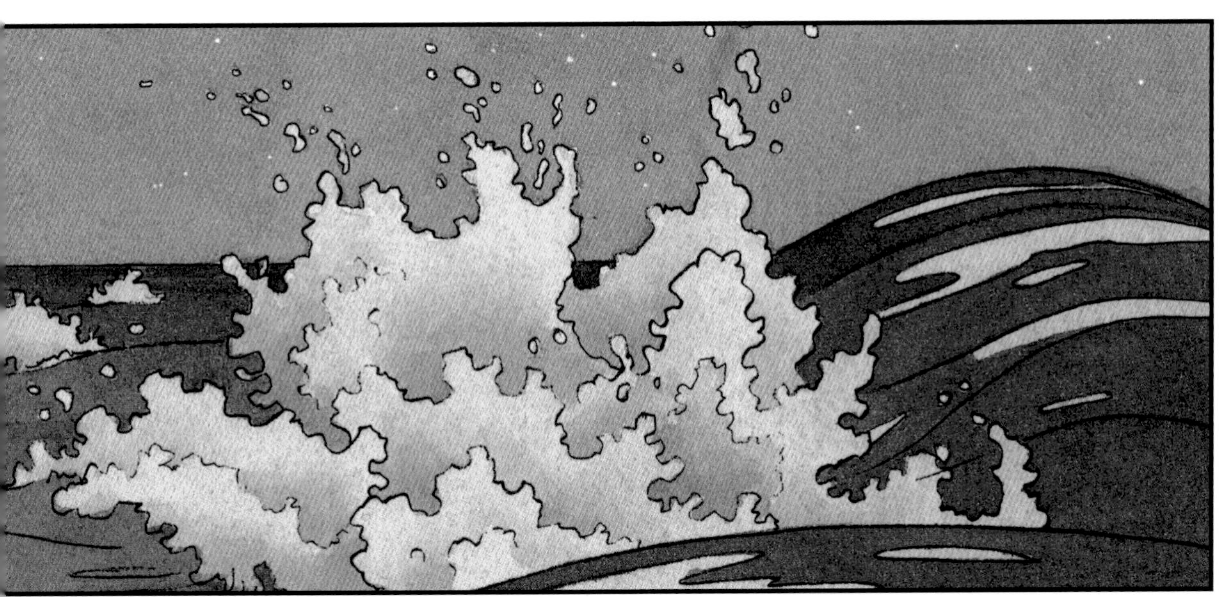

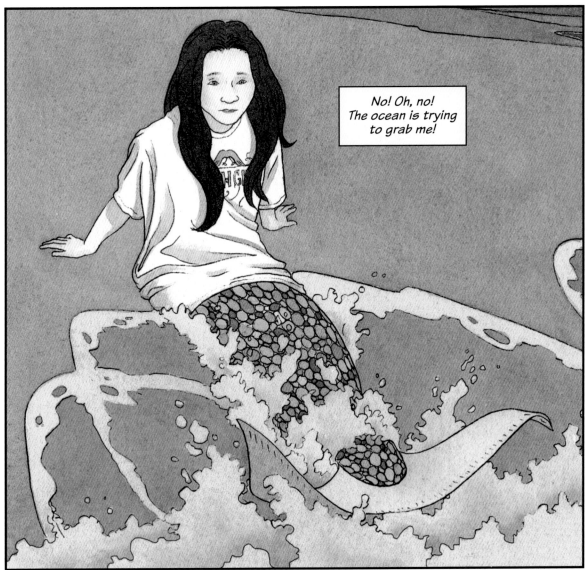

No! Oh, no!
The ocean is trying
to grab me!

Maybe if Octopus came too...

But I would be lost out there. No family...

SO JACK HANDED HER THE SOY SAUCE BY MISTAKE, BECAUSE IT'S DARK, LIKE VINEGAR.
OH, NO! THE GOOF!
YOU SHOULD HAVE SEEN HER FACE WHEN SHE TOOK A BITE OF THAT SALAD!
Kids...like Livia. Like me?

They laugh a lot.

I'd like to laugh like that.
What if I went up to them? What would I say?

That's my home? It seems much bigger inside, but it's really just a speck. It's my cage.

FISH GIRL

Locked!

There must be another way...

Locked too.

Nothing!

Octopus!

Neptune will find me.
I could run away now. Oh,
but I couldn't leave them
behind. It's their cage too.

I could hide. Maybe sneak
in when he opens up.
It might work. I'm so tired.

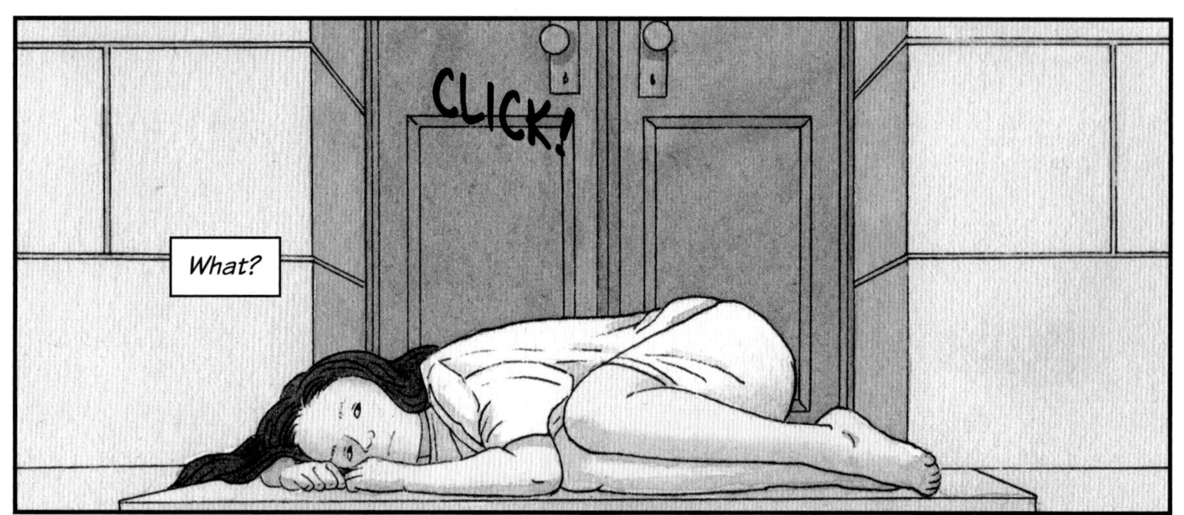
CLICK!
What?

Octopus, you waited up all night for me, didn't you?

I was so scared. It was almost a disaster. But I went out into the world as a girl!

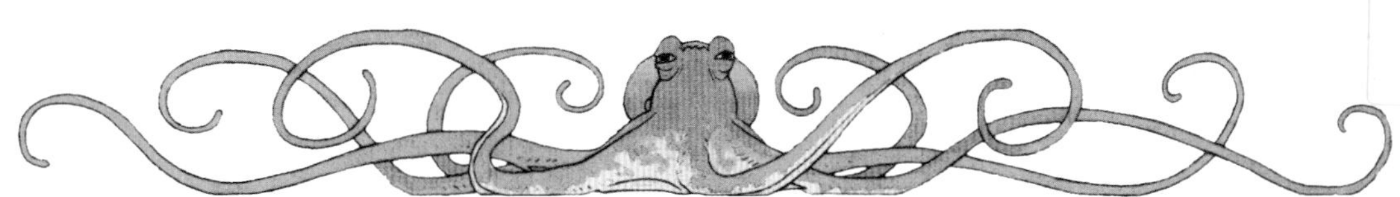

No, Octopus,
I'm too tired.

Oh, okay. I'll play. I don't want him to yell. I'll keep him happy.

THERE! THERE!

I SAW HER!
ME TOO!

LOOK AT THE SIZE OF THAT OCTOPUS!
Livia! Wait till she sees me in my shirt!

FISHGIRL
WHAT?

Do I look awful?

I'M SORRY! I THOUGHT... YOU WERE... REAL.
A GIRL.

DID HE GIVE YOU THAT SHIRT?

NO? SO HOW DID YOU GET IT?

YOU'RE SNEAKY, HUH?

WHAT IF I GAVE YOU SOME CLOTHES? WOULDN'T THAT BE FUN?
I BET YOU AND I ARE THE SAME SIZE. WE COULD SHARE, LIKE SISTERS.

I WANT TO TAKE YOUR PICTURE IN THE SHIRT.

No, no, no! No pictures. That's rule number one.

SORRY!
YOU KNOW, I COULD TRY TO HELP YOU. I COULD TELL...
No! No!
ARE YOU SURE?

I need a way to help my sea friends first.

I CAN'T STAY TODAY. WE'RE GOING TO MY AUNT'S HOUSE. I'LL BE BACK TOMORROW AFTERNOON.
Wait...Don't go.

BYE!
She can come and go whenever she wants.

The day is so long without her.

I'll play his games.

When he's happy, he leaves me alone.

There they go again—showtime.
Octopus, he doesn't want anything
from you except for you to be you.

But you're just as
much a prisoner as
I am. As all of us are.
I wish we were free.

MMMMMMMMMMMMMMMMM

"Storms." Ha.
Liar.

I was good today.
I did what he told me.
I'll get a story.
I want to hear more about my mother. But is anything he says true? What good are a bunch of lies about my mother?

THERE YOU ARE! THAT'S THE WAY TO PLAY IT!
EVERYONE WAS TALKING ABOUT YOU.

DO YOU SEE NOW? BUSINESS DEPENDS ON YOU.

YOU'RE WHAT MAKES US SPECIAL.

YOU HAD ME SO WORRIED, I GOT ABSENT-MINDED...I LEFT THE DOOR UNLOCKED LAST NIGHT.
WELL, EVERYTHING'S OKAY NOW. HOW ABOUT A STORY? YOU EARNED IT!

WHAT?

WHY NOT? COME...

I THOUGHT YOU WERE MY GOOD GIRL AGAIN.
SUIT YOURSELF.

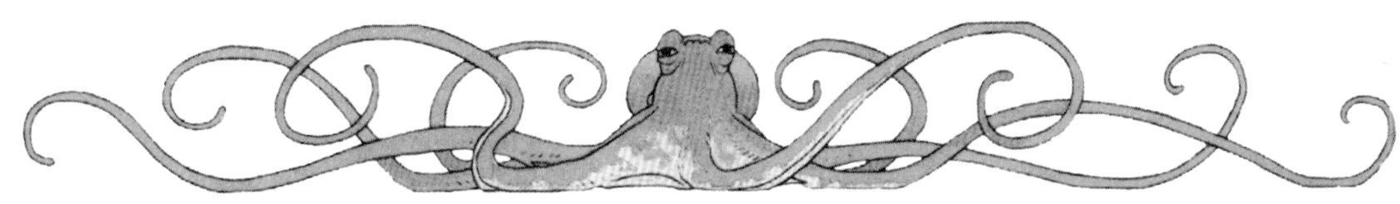

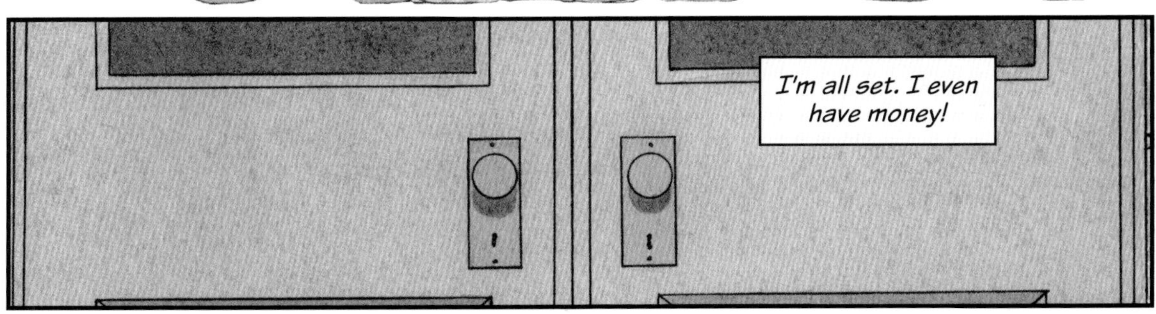
I'm all set. I even have money!

I hope I'll blend in better.

This time I won't get locked out. I can see how to do it. I just push this thing and the door stays unlocked.

It was you the other night, wasn't it? You unlocked the door for me. Down all those stairs...

You understand everything. You always have. I'd never leave you behind.

FISH

only

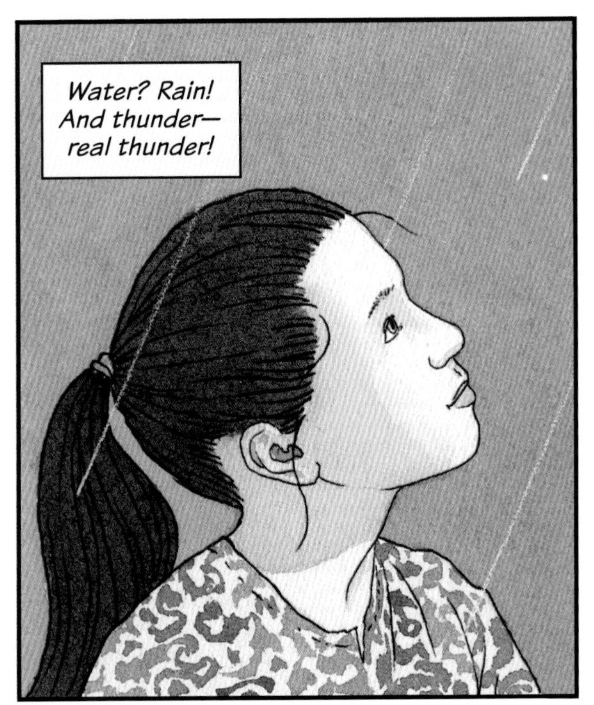
Water? Rain!
And thunder—
real thunder!

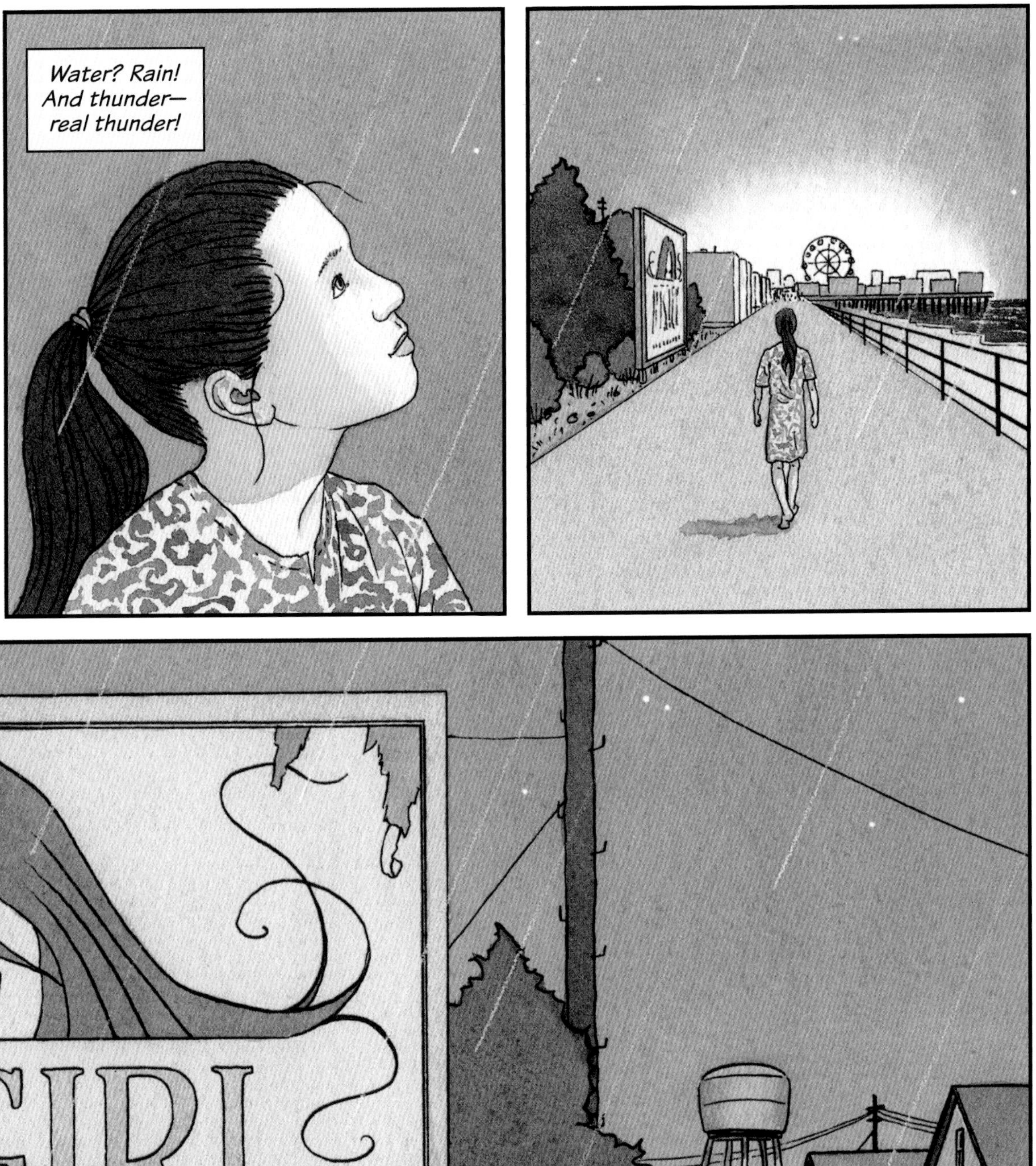

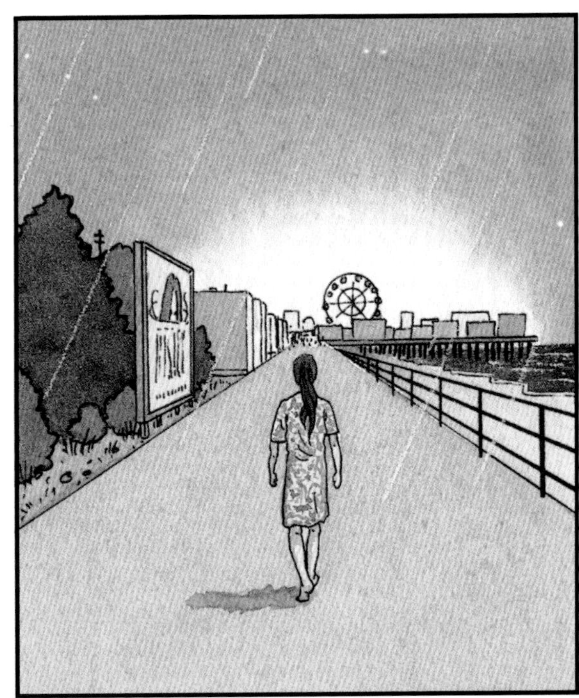

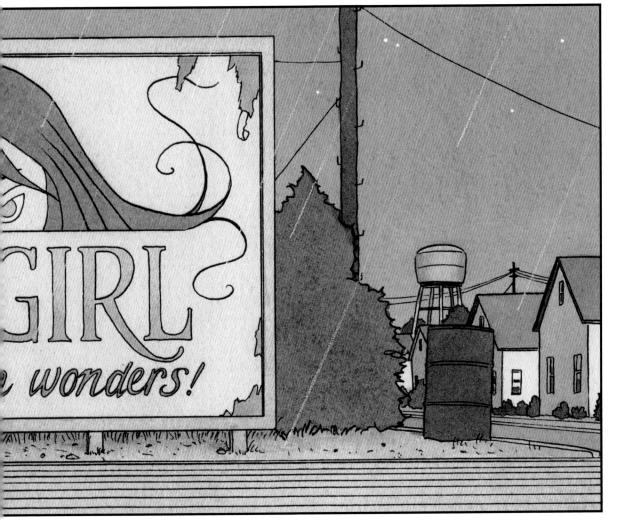

GIRL
wonders!

Oh, my.

So many people!
FUN!

No one notices me.
I'm one of them.

How funny—people want to get out of the rain.

I love it!

Hello, fish!

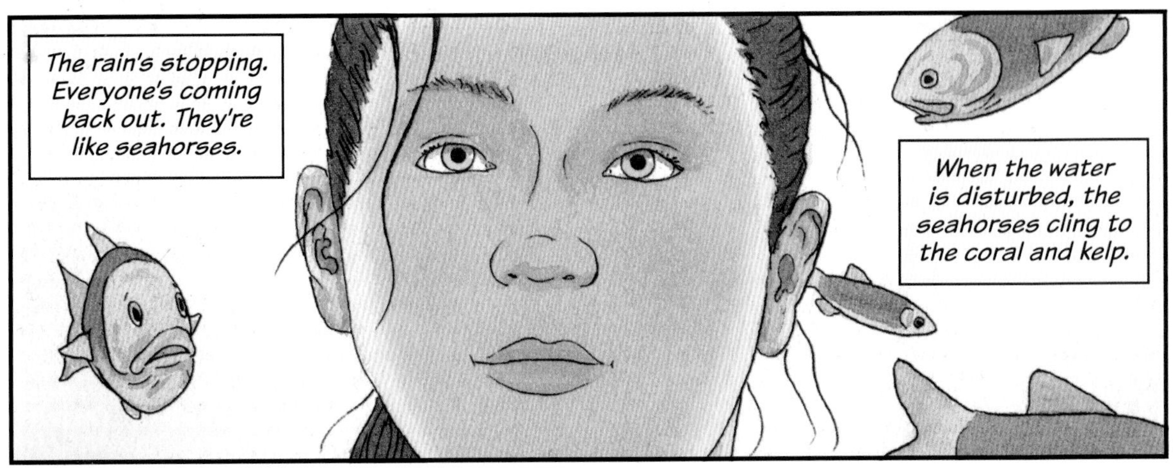
The rain's stopping. Everyone's coming back out. They're like seahorses.
When the water is disturbed, the seahorses cling to the coral and kelp.

But when it calms down, they come drifting out again. People are like that with rain.

Hello!

MOM! MOM, LOOK!

Uh-oh. I have to be careful.

That's peet-zuh.

WHAT CAN I GET FOR YOU, KID?
PIZ

ONE SLICE, COMIN' UP. FRESH AND HOT.

THAT'LL BE TWO FIFTY.
AHEM. TWO FIFTY.
What does he want?

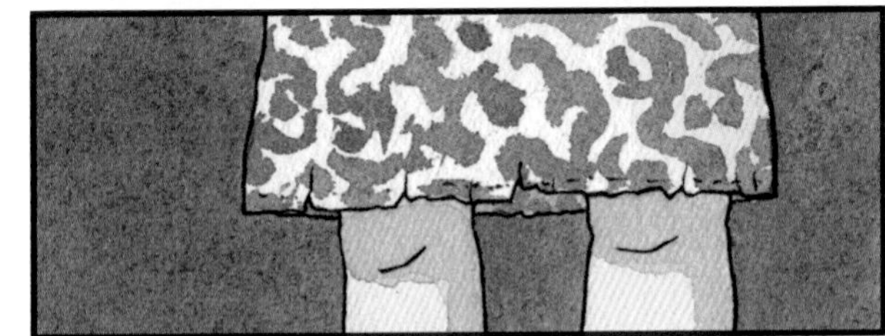

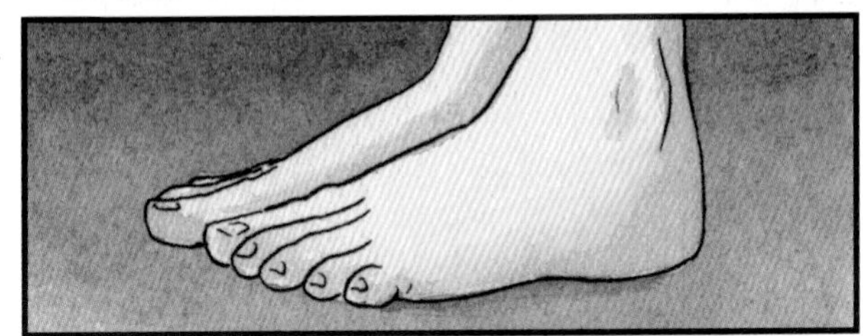

Money! I have it!
I KNOW ABOUT YOU, KID. I SEE RIGHT THROUGH YOU.
PIZ

He's looking at my legs.
He can tell.

YOUR HAIR'S A MESS, THAT OLD DRESS, THE BARE FEET.

DO YOU SPEAK ENGLISH? DO YOU NEED HELP?

I...no.

HEY, COME BACK!
PIZZA

I should go home.
Which way is it?

LOOKING FOR SOMEBODY?

Go away!
YOU'VE GOT NICE HAIR.

AW, I DIDN'T MEAN ANYTHING.
Leave me alone.

THE RAIN'S STARTING UP AGAIN. I'VE GOT A CAR.
Don't!

LOOK AT THOSE ENORMOUS WAVES!
WHOA!

C'MON. LET'S GET OUT OF HERE—
NO!

LOOK OUT!
IS IT A TSUNAMI?

The ocean is watching me. It wants me back.

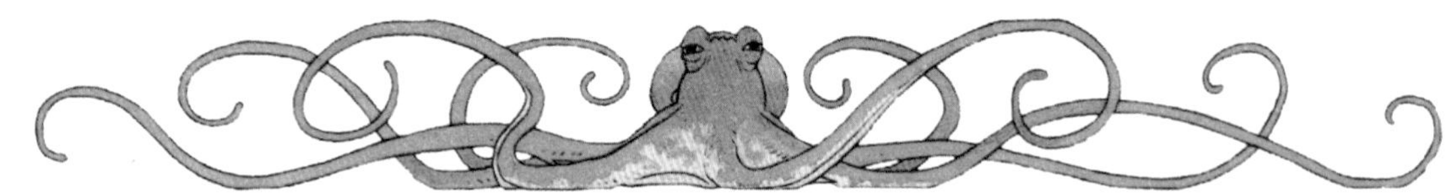

Ouch!

Stop playing around.

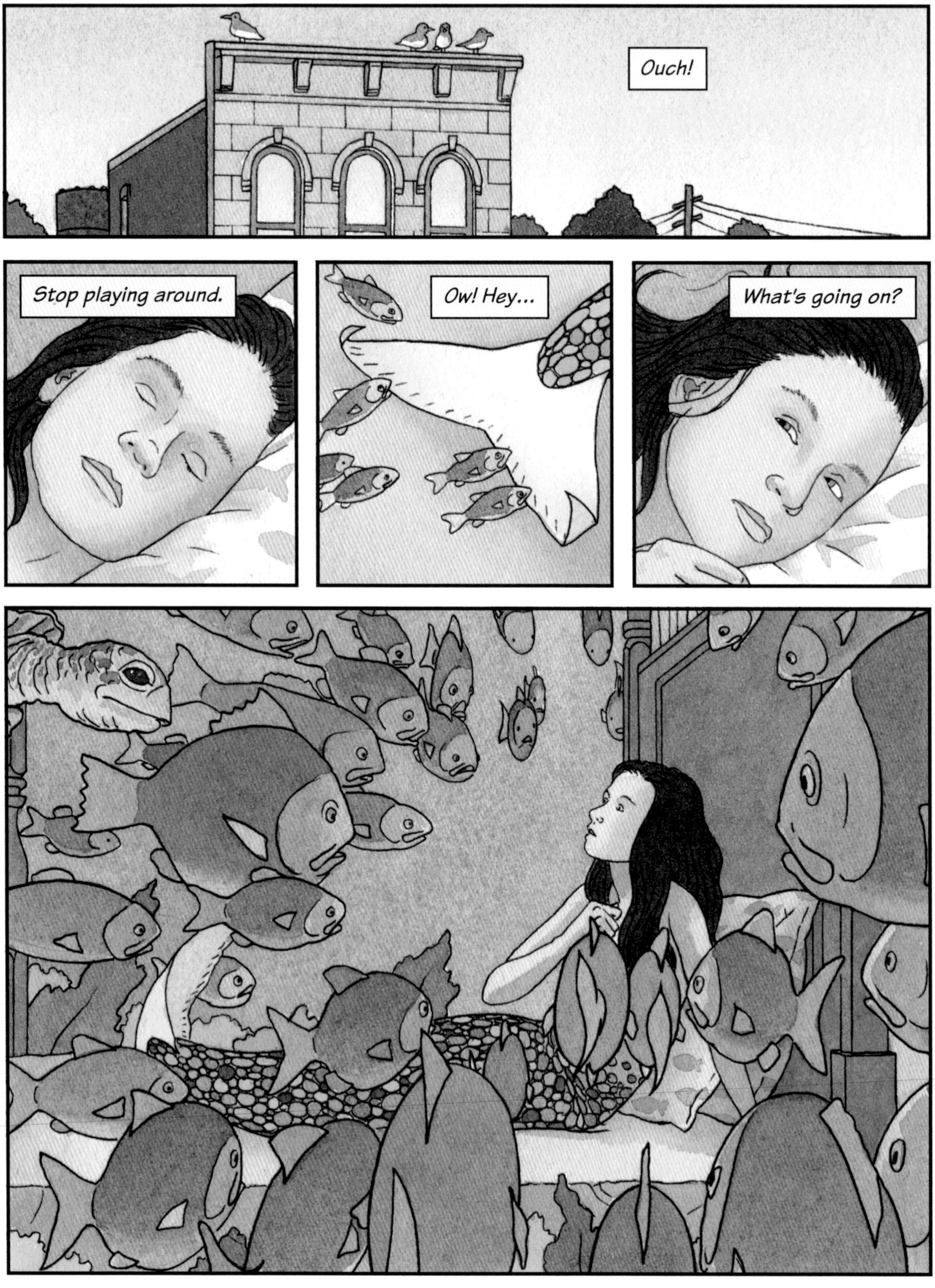

Ow! Hey...

What's going on?

What's the matter
with all of you?

Turtle! Not you too?

What did
I do?

Octopus, what's
happening?

Why are the fish afraid? You and Shark aren't. Oh, no!

Octopus! He'll kill you!

You did it!

Thank you.
At least **you** still love me.

The aquarium is opening.

How can we play the game anyhow?

The fish won't help me hide anymore.

They don't recognize me. I'm no longer one of them. I've lost them.

Where is Livia?
I hope she gets
here soon.

I'm ready for her.

At last!

A DRESS!

HEY!

YOU MADE IT INTO A NECKLACE.

IS THAT FOR ME?

IT'S BEAUTIFUL. I LOVE IT. I'LL WEAR IT TO MY SWIM CLASS.
You swim?

WHAT'S THAT LOOK?

WHERE ARE YOU GOING?

Good...

...he'll be busy for a while.

WHAT'S GOING ON?

YOU WANT ME TO COME INTO THE TANK?

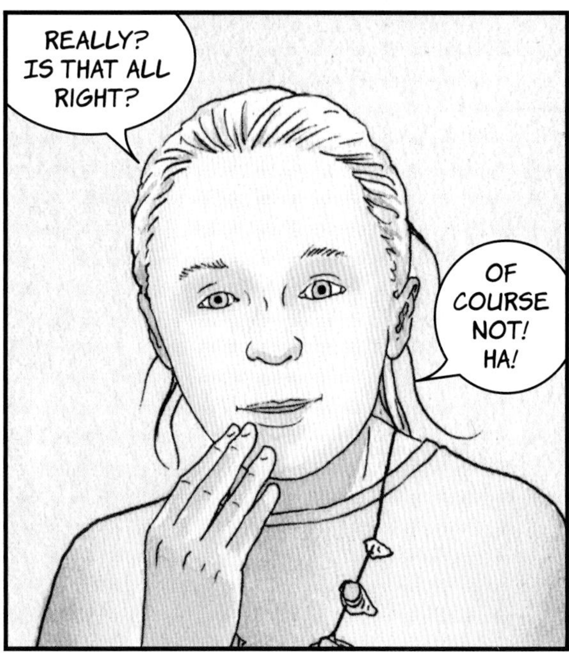
REALLY? IS THAT ALL RIGHT?
OF COURSE NOT! HA!

HOLD IT—
CAN THAT
SHARK GET IN
THERE?

No.
ARE YOU
SURE?

REALLY?
OKAY...

WHOA!
WHAT ABOUT
THAT GUY?

*She's my friend.
Our friend. Here—
feel her arm.*
OOH...
SUCTION
CUPS.

IT'S COLD IN HERE, LIKE THE OCEAN.
SOMEHOW I THOUGHT IT WOULD BE LIKE A POOL. HEATED, YOU KNOW?

I'M SUCH A GOOF! YOU'VE NEVER FELT A HEATED POOL.

COME ON, LET'S SWIM!

I WISH YOU
COULD TALK
TO ME.

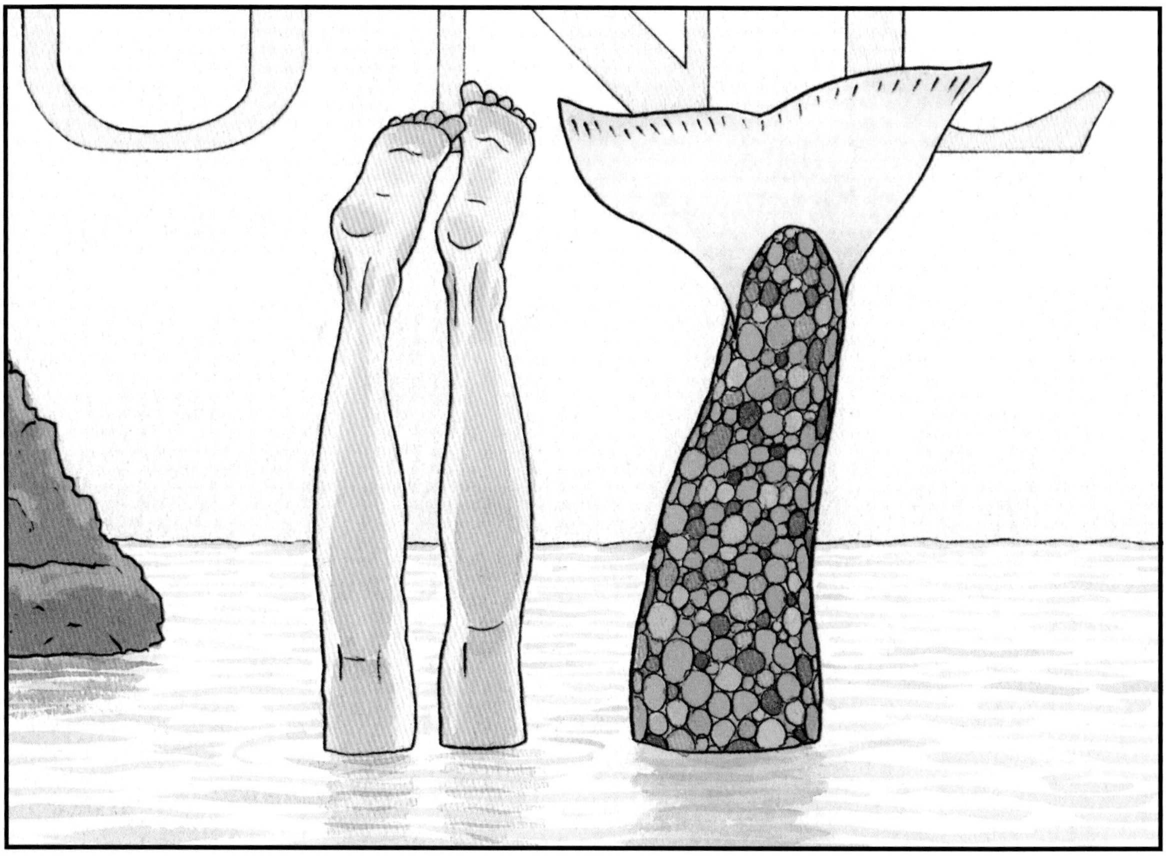

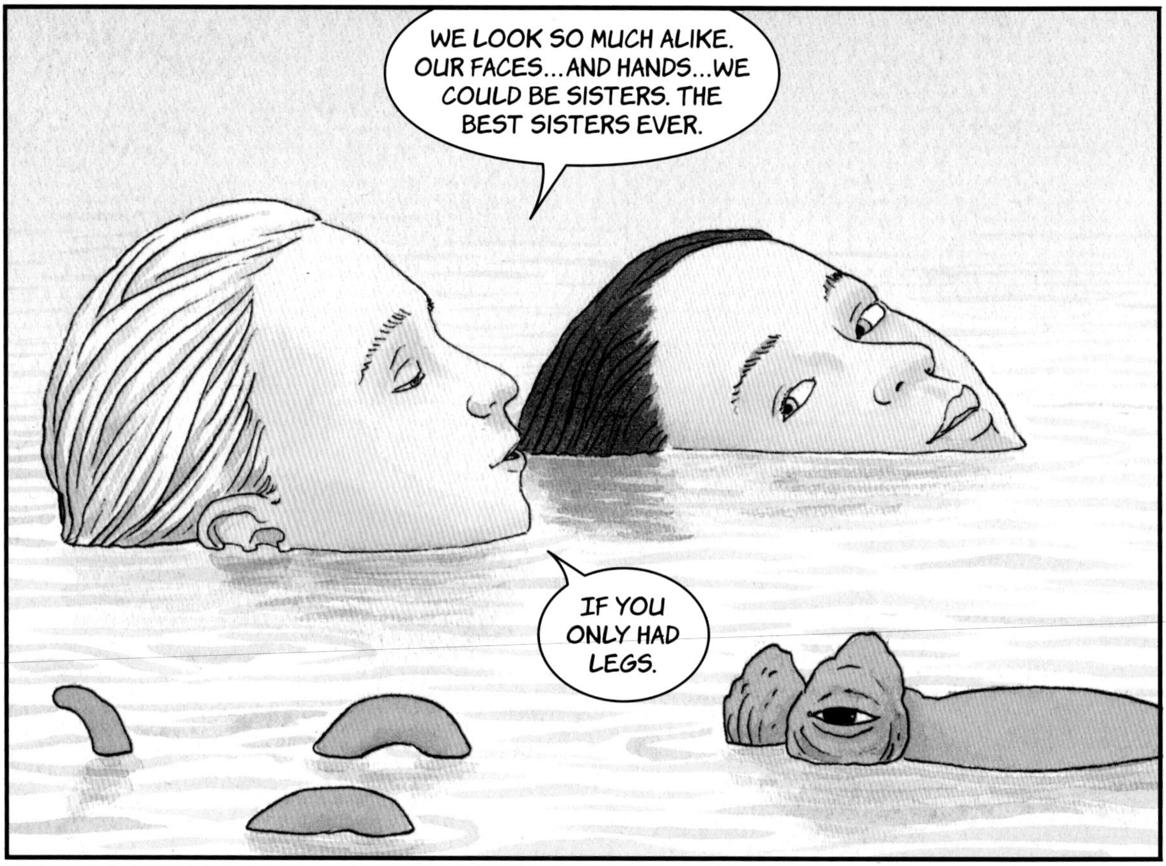

WE LOOK SO MUCH ALIKE. OUR FACES...AND HANDS...WE COULD BE SISTERS. THE BEST SISTERS EVER.

IF YOU ONLY HAD LEGS.

I do!

WHERE ARE YOU GOING?
Just watch.

WHAT IS THIS!?

GET OUT! GET OUT OR YOU'LL BE SORRY.

I'LL SCREAM!

JUST TRY IT!

I'LL DEAL WITH YOU LATER.
My fault. All my fault.

SHE'S A PRISONER! I'M GOING TO TELL.
TELL? TELL WHAT? YOU SAW A MERMAID? THEY'LL LAUGH AT YOU.

I DON'T BELIEVE YOU. YOU WOULDN'T DARE!
ANYWAY, BY THE TIME YOU COME BACK, THERE WON'T BE ANYTHING TO TELL ABOUT.

YOU HAVE NO IDEA WHAT I'LL DO. NOW GET GOING.

AND DON'T TELL. DON'T DO THAT TO HER.

BYE, MIRA.
MY FRIEND.

Goodbye, friend.

SHE GAVE YOU A NAME?
Yes.

I CAN'T BELIEVE THIS.
YOU FOOL! YOU'VE RUINED US.

DON'T YOU SEE? SHE'LL TALK FOR SURE. THE AUTHORITIES WILL COME.

THEY'LL TAKE YOU AWAY.

IS THAT WHAT YOU WANT? TO LEAVE ME?
Yes.

THEY WON'T TREASURE YOU LIKE I DO.

WHOOOOSSSSHHHH

THAT STORM CAME UP FAST.

I CAN FIGURE THIS OUT.
YOU CAN HIDE BEFORE THEY COME. YES...
THEY'LL TAKE ME AT MY WORD.
This has to stop.

I JUST NEED TO...

WHAT?

NO!

HOW COULD YOU DO THIS TO ME?

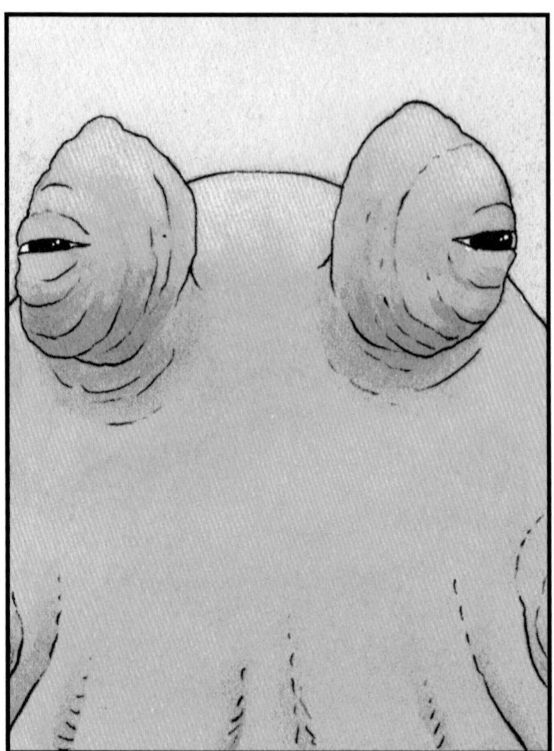

YOU BETRAYED ME!
You lied to me.

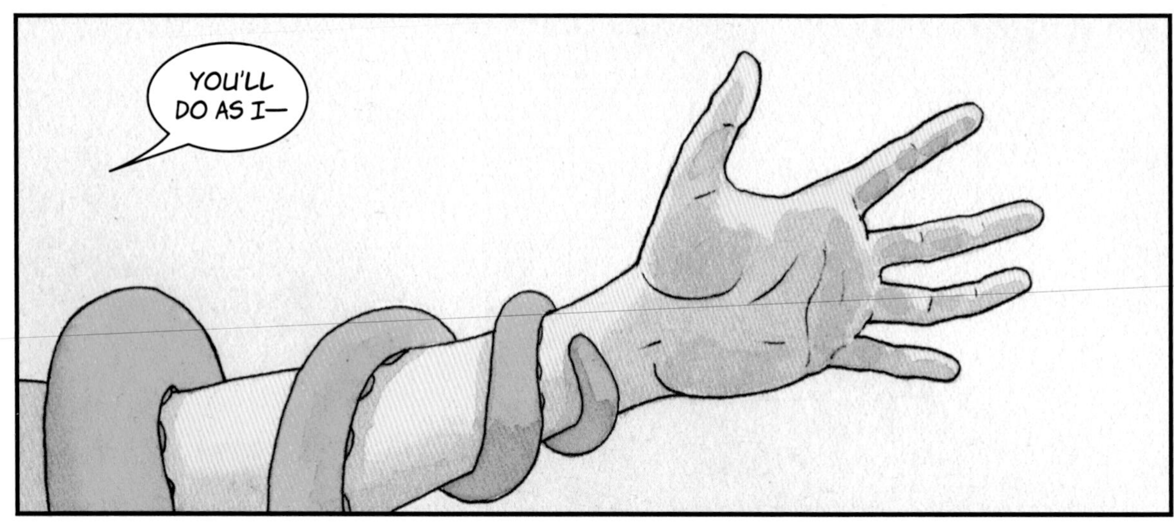
YOU'LL DO AS I—

YOU TOO?

The lights!

THAT GIRL CAN'T HELP YOU!

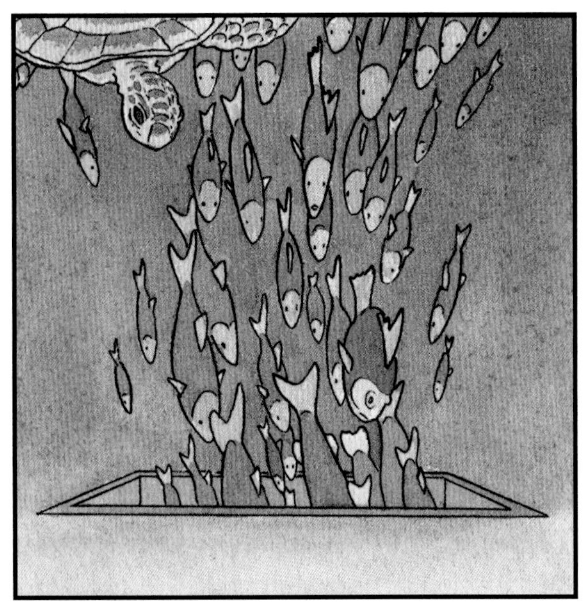

GO AHEAD, RUN!

YOU CAN'T SURVIVE WITHOUT ME.

SNAP!

FISH

Take them back!
They belong to you!

Go! You're free!

Stop! Not the town—
just this prison!

Please! Stop the storm!

It's dying down.
You listened.
Thank you, ocean.
My ocean. My home.
MYSTERIOUS

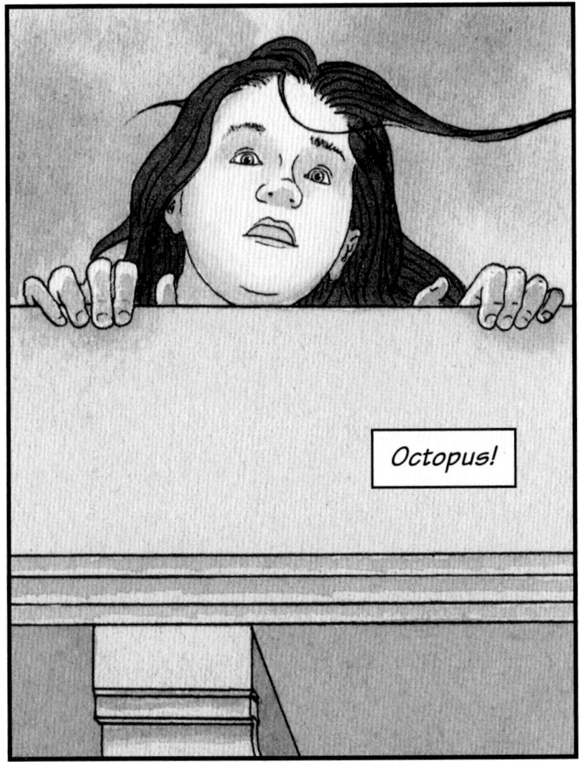
Octopus!

Tear this place down!

SEE THE MYSTERIOUS
FISH GIRL
WHO IS SHE ? WHAT IS SHE
VISIT
OCEAN
WOND

I have no choice.

Where's my tail?

I'm sinking.
I can't breathe!

I'm drowning.
That's funny!
A mermaid
drowning...

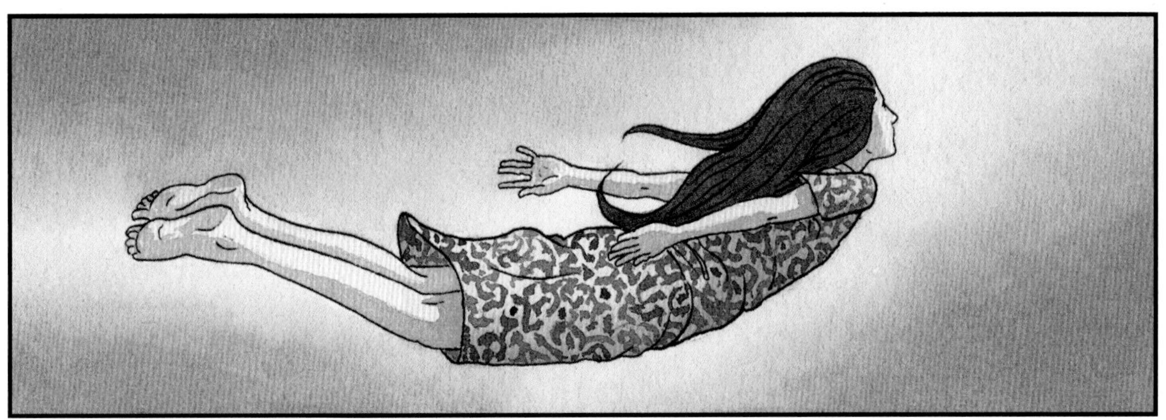

Oh! You're sending me back.

I'm not your child.
You aren't my home.
This is what I want.

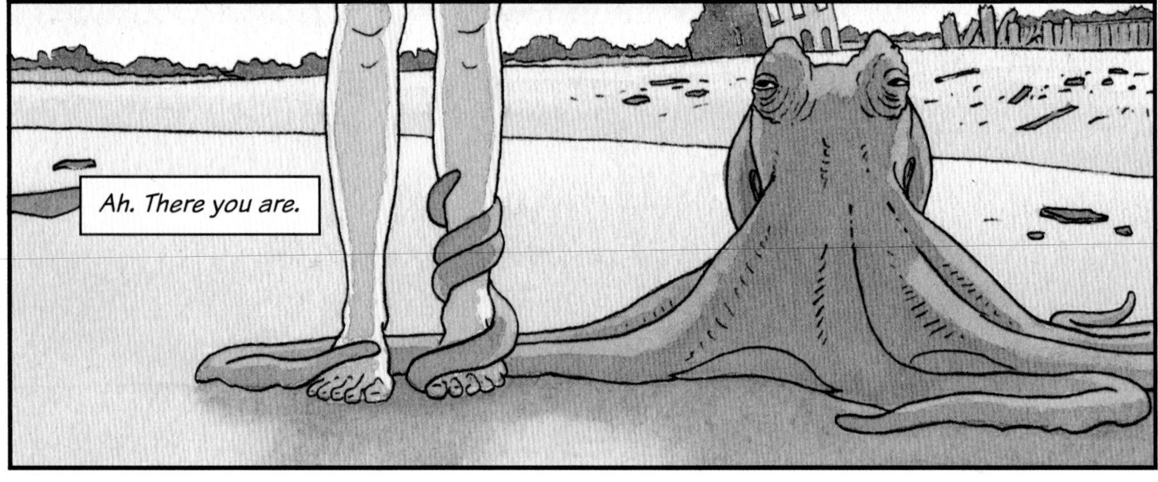

Octopus, I'll miss you so, so much. Dear friend.

We are free. Goodbye.

FISH
SHE BREATHES
THAT'S MY DOGHOUSE. IT GOT WASHED ALL THE WAY OUT HERE.
HAVEN'T SEEN A STORM THAT BAD IN YEARS. LIKE A HURRICANE, BUT FASTER.

HAS ANYONE SEEN A BLUE TABLE WITH A STRIPED UMBRELLA?

SO, WERE YOU THE ONLY ONE IN THERE?
Neptune!

ANY OTHER EMPLOYEES?

HEY, BUDDY, YOU LISTENING?
WHAT? NO. THERE WAS NO ONE ELSE INSIDE.

That's Livia!

APPARENTLY, THAT GIRL KNEW SOMEONE WHO WORKED IN THERE.
NO ONE IN THAT HOUSE COULD HAVE SURVIVED. POOR KID.
COME ON, HONEY.

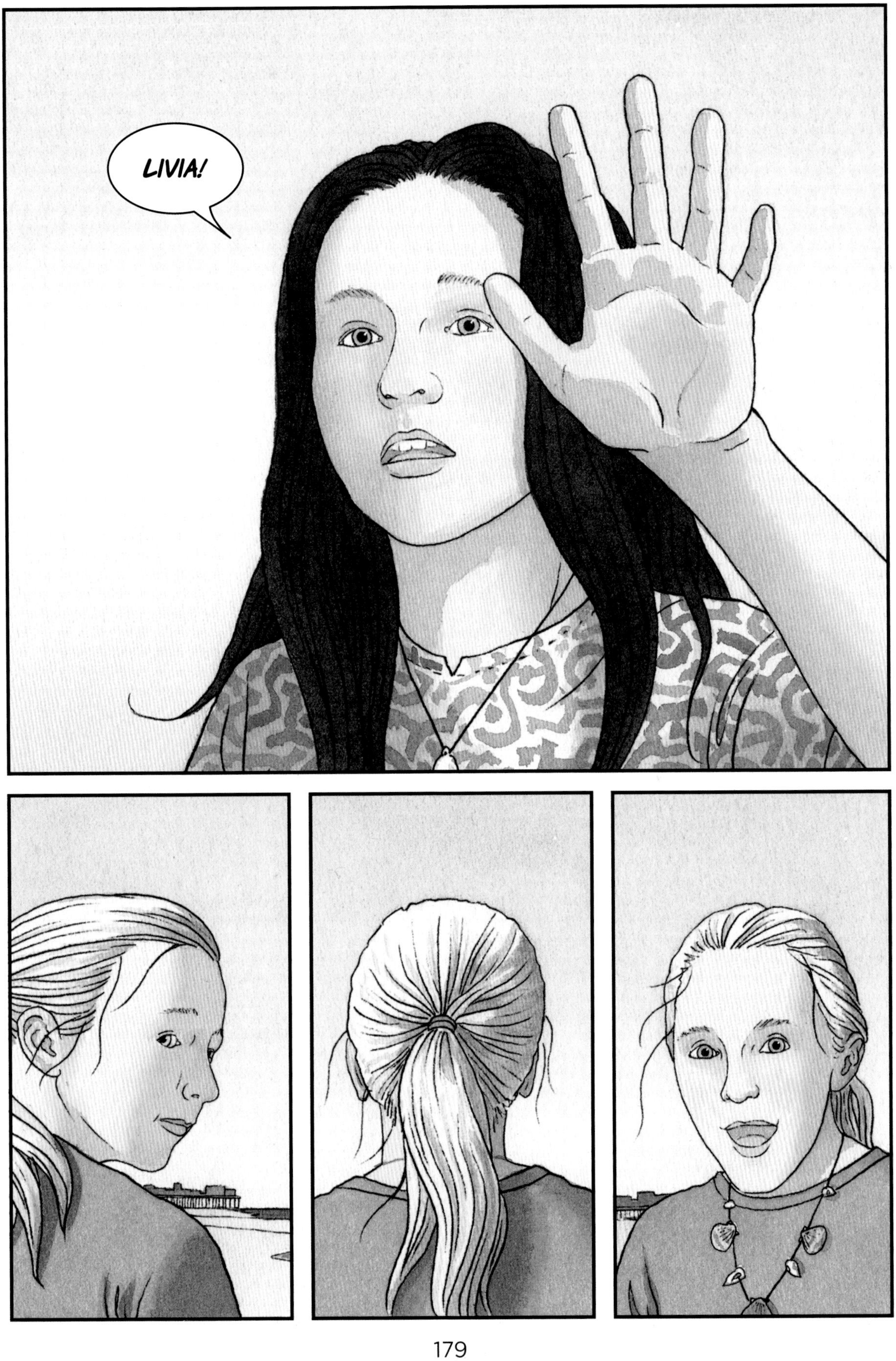

LIVIA!

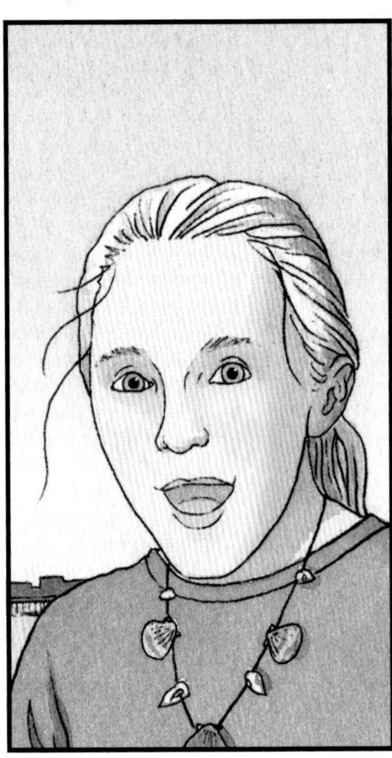

MIRA!

IT'S YOU!
AND YOU'VE GOT LEGS! HOW DID...
OH, WHO CARES!

LIVIA.
MIRA.